MEET ME IN PRAGUE

MEET ME IN PRAGUE

GEORGE CABANAS

Bubba Conch Press

This is a work of fiction. All of the characters, organizations, and events portrayed in this book are either products of the author's imagination or are used fictitiously.

Cover Art: Bubba Conch Press

Published by Bubba Conch Press
Oviedo, FL

An Imprint of Salt Ponds Publishing, LLC

ISBN 978-1-971454-00-9 (paperback)
ISBN 978-1-971454-01-6 (e-book)
ISBN 978-1-971454-02-3 (audio book)

AI Disclaimer: Some of the images featured in this book were created using generative artificial intelligence, based solely on the author's original descriptions. No part of the story, its characters, or narrative was written or composed by AI.

Bubba Conch Press maintains a strict AI policy: all published fiction and non-fiction must be the creative work of human authors, and significant AI-generated storytelling or character creation is not permitted.

Bubba Conch Press

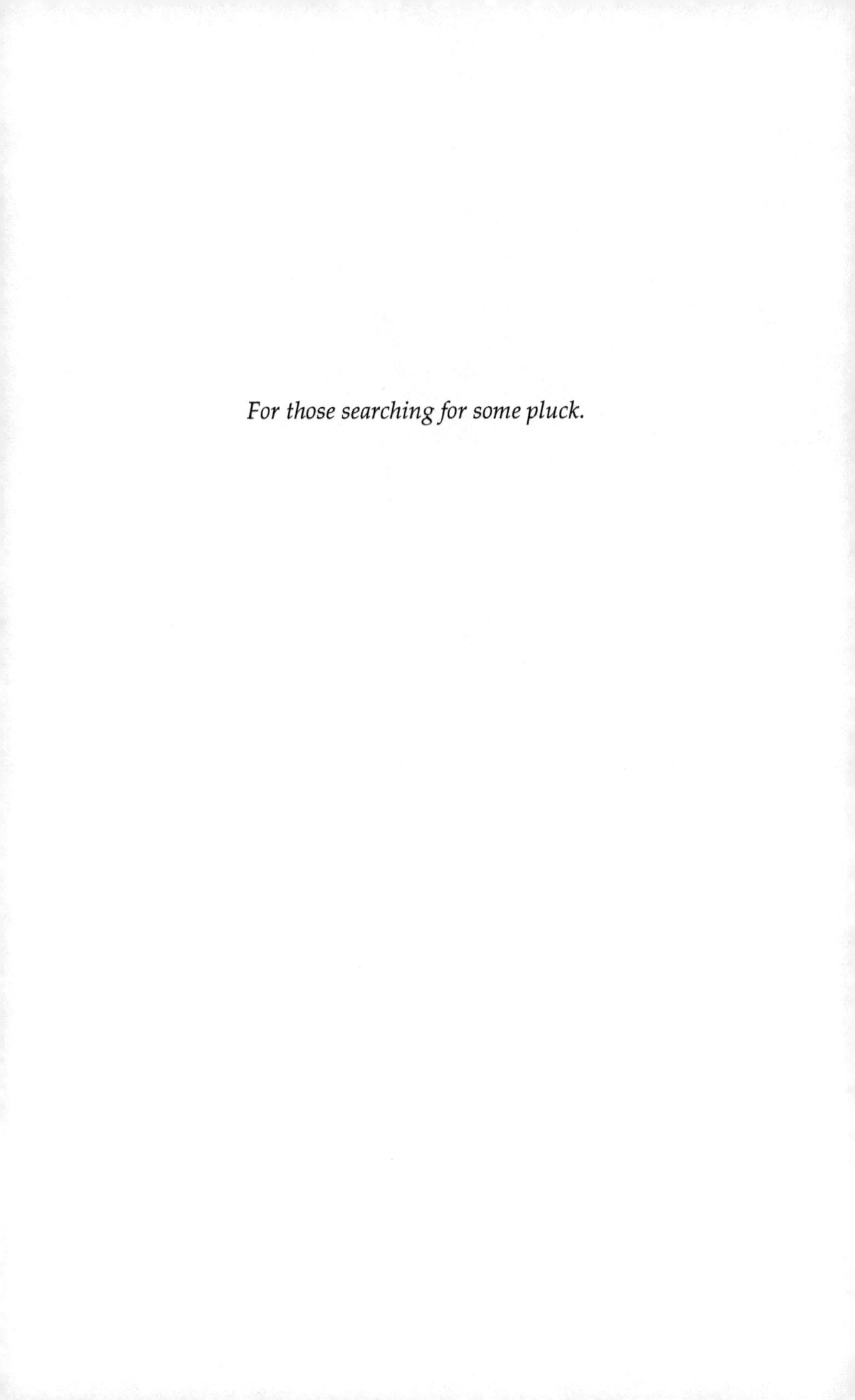

For those searching for some pluck.

But if he only lives twenty-one days, he will find out that only those rare natures that are made up of pluck, endurance, devotion to duty for duty's sake, and invincible determination may hope to venture upon so tremendous an enterprise as the keeping of a journal and not sustain a shameful defeat.

- Mark Twain, Innocents Abroad

1

PROLOGUE

"This is the final boarding for KLM flight 1609 to Amsterdam, Gate B12." The thick Czech accent echoed through the concourse. I never fully learned one of these European languages, but I love the dark sound of the muffled, rolling tongue in the central and eastern countries. Alphabet letters that look like my own, but with ticks and accent marks orbiting the familiar shapes. A year ago, I wouldn't have had such a fascination with these types of things. I don't think I had anything of wonder at all but my lust for indecisiveness. But here I am, standing in front of this newsstand at Vaclav Havel Airport gladly emptying my pockets of my last 500 Koruna—paper painted with a rose-colored flower with the face of some historic figure staring into the distance. Several months ago, I would have figured this to be an ounce of gold in my hand, but I am keen on the fact it is more like two Cokes, a bag of chips, and some gum. Behind me, masses of people create a vortex of sounds. Delightful things. People. When you least expect it, they do something incredibly memorable. For example, the young mother stopping to check beyond the fabric veil obscuring the face of her child. What is she looking for exactly? The text on the child's face, of course. It's remarkable to me that one day this toddler will forget the attentiveness of these moments. However, at this instance of time, there is a smile lighting up the walls of the concourse. A work of art. Delightful.

A step closer to the counter now. I'm practicing the Czech word for "hello" in my head, barely moving my lips. I know when the time comes, I will freeze. I will be infantile and just smile at the charming clerk peeking around the veil of the customer in front of me to see my face. Delightful.

"*Dobrý den,*" that stubby, hard "r" enchants me every time.

"Doe-bree din," I'm embarrassed for myself. I knew I would blow it. I take it as best as I can because I tried. My eyes track to the floor, my head shaking in soft self-disapproval. A restrained giggle.

"Will that be all?"

Ah! I have the perfect Czech response for this one, "*Ano,*" which is to say, "yep" in the foreign tongue. Nailed it!

2

HANGOUTS

F*ive Years Before*

"Oh yeah, you nailed it!" Jacob's eyes roll and pause.

"Shut up, dude," I grasp my knee. However, the primary pain is pulsing from my pride. "Let's see you do it."

"Me?"

"Yes…you." I do not expect him to do it. I'm just stalling for time to allow my ego to pick itself off the cafeteria floor.

"Nah. I have bad knees or something. Besides, I am not the one who said I could jump from table to table." No, he didn't say that, I did. "Oops." A sinister smile appears on Jacobs's face.

In my mind, I replay Jacob's "oops." Oops? Oops, about what?

"Mr. Lopez…again." Crap. I can smell the aroma of coffee and jelly beans. Mr. Beady, the dean. "Mr. Beady! I was just thinkin' abouchya." A barely hidden lie. I would say at least fifty percent of my high school experience was lying to Mr.

Beady. He always seemed to be present when I did anything remotely chaotic. One time Jacob dared me to tie a gym sock around my head and run through the breezeway yelling, "Something smells like feet!" I made it all the way to the end when Mr. Beady appeared from behind the corner. He inquired what I was doing, and I replied that I had forgotten to take my meds. He was not amused.

Mr. Beady was not really too bad of a guy. I guess my biggest complaint is he never showed any emotion. He was hard to read. His thin lips concealed any hint of a smile; any hint of sadness; any hint of pain. They were just parallel pieces of flesh dangling underneath his pig nose, scabs of an ancient organ that used to have some evolutionary purpose but now is rarely used. My friends called him "Tommy Hawk", a clever combination of my name and our school mascot: The Tomahawks.

"Mr. Lopez, why do you always seem to be acting a fool?"

My shoulders shrug and I mumble, "Don't know."

"Uh, uh. I see. Well, how does thinking about it in detention sound?" I swear his lips did not move.

"Mr. Beady, I–"

"I'm going to stop you right there. Same place. Same time." Into the shadows, he disappears.

Jacob looking at me with those stupid sunken eyes makes a gesture as if he is throwing a tomahawk at me. "Dude, that sucks, bro. How many times has he 'hawked' you this year? One hundred or something?"

"No, not a hundred, idiot. Probably like ninety-three or so."

The thing about Jacob is that I could never stay mad at him for very long. He was a good friend. I can't deny that he was a bit obnoxious and probably attention-hungry. I think we all would have if we wore his shoes. Jacob was basically raising himself. He had no idea who his father was and several years ago his mother died from cancer. Jack, his step-father, agreed to let Jacob stay in the house but he was always gone and never completely warmed up to Jacob as a father figure. Jacob was always a bit of a lost soul—a sweet, friendly, and lost soul. Without Jacob, my high school experience would have been much different.

"Are you going to Stoner's tonight?"

"I think so. Who's going?

"Pretty much the whole gang from what everyone is saying. I think Katrina is bringing her *puto*, too."

TIGHT, curly hair and soft dark olive skin. A stunning smile that beamed sunshine whenever she laughed at one of my jokes. Katrina. My helpless curiosity began the moment I met her. A straight "A" student and the vice president of the Math Club. Every time I see her, I am in anguish within myself. She's my dream debutante. I made every excuse to find ways to spend time with her. "I need help with my homework." That was a favorite tactic of mine. Her father died serving with the Army in Afghanistan and her mother remarried to an awful human being, a situation of which I took selfish advantage. I'm not proud of it. Abusive and out-of-control, Andy Edinburgh lashed out at Katrina's mother Jane regularly. Sometimes the subjective arrows of drunken words led to real physical violence. Katrina often shielded her mother from the onslaught. I became her emotional outlet and confidant. Often, I would wish at night Andy was giving them a hard time so she would call me or offer me an opportunity to give her consoling hugs the next day. I'm not sure I will ever forgive myself for those criminal thoughts. In my shallow defense, hearing her voice or feeling her touch was like a drug to me. I was willing to be morally valueless in the conflict because I valued her above almost all else. The battles won came at a high price.

I never told her how I felt, though I would tear up thinking about her before I fell asleep. One day, when I was under the delusion that I had courage, I wrote her a corny poem.

Katrina, I know you are my friend
Without you, my life would end
I love the way you smell
Help me to end this living hell
Katrina, I would buy you a red rose
At the hardware store a garden hose
I am not sure you ever knew
Katrina, I love you.

EMBARRASSING. Terrible. I'm not a poet. I do not believe a single part of me is. I'm glad I lost whatever moxie I thought I had. For the time, it was the best I could muster. It wasn't anything but a forgettable attempt.

I OBSCURE the emotion inside of me. "Oh. Okay. Cool. Whatever."

The moment breaks with a voice yelling across the cafeteria. "What's goin' on, Tommy, Tommy, Tommy?"

"Kyyyyyyraaaaaa!" I jump up and down to ridiculous proportions like there is lava beneath my feet, an inside joke.

"Did you guys hear about what happened with Katrina and Deron?"

I shrug my shoulders and try to act like it is no big deal. Jacob and I look at each other and he answers for us, "No. What?"

"Well, I told her he was a dick. I warned her. They broke up. He told her he wanted to see other people. Dick." Kyra never liked any of Katrina's boyfriends—neither did I. She is as happy as I am. I play it cool.

"She was too good for him anyways." The lump in my throat changes the air pressure coming out of my mouth.

"Dude! Here's your chance!" Jacob knew how I felt; Kyra only had her suspicions. I glance at Jacob with a muted look on my face. Red cheeks. Veins bubbled on my neck. A sick feeling rumbled in my guts.

"What? What are you talkin' about?" A pathetic deflection.

"Wait…wait…wait! You have a thing for Katrina?" The fear came back to me. Now Kyra was going to kick my ass.

"Nooooo! Jacob is just playing around. It's, uh, a dumb joke." Kyra pierces through my skin straight to the outer walls of my soul with those voodoo-green eyes. My thoughts scramble and trip over rushing adrenaline. I think, "This witch can smell my deceit."

"Okaaaay? Whatever." Whew! She is buying it. "Any watchasays, I'm going to hunt him down and bury him in a shallow grave. Any willing accomplices?"

Jacob and I giggle nervously. Kyra just might do it. Tension is forming as if we are in a B-horror movie and some cheesy masked murderer is lurking underneath the tables in the cafeteria. *Bing, bong*. Oh, thank lunch-time Jesus, the bell rang. I quickly scurry off and over my shoulder, I yell back, "I'll be at Stoner's tonight! Later!"

Clash! "Mr. Lopez, what are you doing?" Of course, I have run smack into Tommyhawk.

"I don't want to be late to class, Mr. Beady!" I stumble

around him sheepishly but keep moving. "I will see ya after school, right?" Now I'm looking over my other shoulder. *Bam!* The door.

"Keep your eyes forward and stop running before you hurt someone!" Mr. Beady's voice sweeps away like a passing freight train whistle.

I can hear Jacob interject far in the background, "Nailed it!"

3

PENNIES

My mother is a kind soul. She works as a receptionist in a doctor's office–a pediatrician. Plain looking. I wish she would take care of herself better. The pictures on the mantle reflect a skinny, long-haired brunette with a hopeful face. Now, she is worn out and looking towards menopause and an expanding waistline—a heck of thing to think about your mother. When I was a child she would tell me about all the places she wanted to travel: Egypt, Japan, Australia, Norway. "One day soon," she would say, "your father and will take me and see the world!" There was just one major obstacle in her way. A steep mountain of slippery stone, cold beer, and always-ready-to-spit excuses. A balding chunk of flesh I call my dad.

My dad is also a kind soul. A kind, cheap, penny-pinching soul. Everything has a price too steep for my dad. He once aggressively bargained with a gentle older home-owner at a garage sale. He insisted she give him a "buy one, get two free" deal on boxes of candles. Candles. Fifty-cent birthday candles. When I told him that worked out to just over 16 cents for each box, he said he had buyer's remorse. He has a pretty good job, too. He works in finance–the irony is not lost on me. He spends about $2 million a month of the company's money without blinking one of those squinty eyes. With the family budget he is a different person. He barely spends money on anything that is not as he says, "worth its weight in George Washingtons."

Growing up, my parents rarely argued. When they did, it was usually because of some unexpected expense or a surprise increase on a utility bill. Once I had asked to join the Scouts. My parents sat at the table for what seemed like hours and finally, they both resigned and said there was no money. My mother missed her sister's wedding because there was no money. My dad declines an annual fishing trip with his cousin because there is no money. I was once convinced my feet would be chopped to a smaller size when I needed bigger shoes because there was no money. No money. *Wegotnomunie.* I thought that was our last name until I was 12.

"Mom, I am going to Stoner's tonight with everyone."

"Who's everyone?" I detest this futile investigation she does every time I say I am going somewhere. Ignoring her will not work.

"Everyone. My friends." Involuntary eye rolls and a wobbly jaw are my weakness.

"Don't you roll your eyes at me, Mr. Lopez, I will make you stare at your brain for the rest of your life if you keep it up."

Control. I need more control. "Sorry, Stoner, Jacob, Kyra, um, Katrina, and, uh, Pierre. Everyone."

"When do you think you will be home?" She opens an opportunity on this one.

"I don't know, maw. There are going to be girls, boobs and booze, probably some meth and machine guns…"

"You think that is funny?"

"Yep."

"I really miss you being my sweet little boy, not this teenage filth mouth. That's not funny. Do you know what that stuff does to people? You wanna try that again?" I'm giving her that dumb teenage boy look. You know, the one that says, "I know everything" but also "I don't know shit," all at the same time? That look.

"I'm just kidding! But I will probably spend the night. We are going to have a bonfire and I am sure we will all crash there."

She bites her bottom-right lip. That means, "Okay, but I don't like it." She permits me and I give her a big hug.

Dad waltzes into the room. He has heard the whole conversation. "You need a condom?"

Mom gasps. "For what!?"

"Mosquitoes. What do you think?"

"He is too young to be doing all of that!" Her face is flush with blood rushing to her cheeks.

Dad shakes his head and turns to walk back out of the room. As he clears the doorway he sarcastically mutters, "Yeah, because you didn't do any of that stuff when you were his age, right, Mother Teresa?"

"Shut the hell up, sicko!" She is as bright as a radiating beacon set on top of a hill. "Your father is just saying stuff. You keep that thing put away, mister. You are too young." She adds, "And remember: God is watching you!" I am looking at her face, but I am ignoring her. Now that they have had a lengthy conversation about it—though never saying the actual word—my mind is going to Katrina and images of her in a bikini from last summer.

"How is Katrina doing?"

"Who?" Shame consumes me. Can she read my thoughts?

"Katrina. How is she?" Mom always liked Katrina.

"Okay, I guess. Her and what's his name broke up today. She said she is still going tonight. So, I guess she is doing alright." Of course, the sinister Cretan within me is hoping she is devastated so I can be her hero.

"Is that right? Are you going to ask her out?"

"What? No. Why would I do that? That's lame."

"I was just asking. You talk about her all of the time." This is true. It's best to leave my denial floating in the air and not add to the uncomfortable moment. I walk away.

My dad is sitting on the floor messing around with the legs of a chair. He is already entering the cursing stage. Time is short. "*¡Viejo!*"

My dad's head drops slightly so he can see above the glass of his readers. "*¡Dime, papacito!*" After he says this, he continues in light obscenity at the chair under his breath.

"Can I get a few dollars for tonight?"

His motion stops. "For what?"

"Just a few dollars in case we do something. I don't know." I admit my negotiation skills are not spectacular.

"Go out back and take a few dollars from the money tree…oh, wait, it doesn't grow on trees."

"Funny. Come on, Dad, don't be such a tightwad."

"Don't you have a job?"

"You know I don't work for Papa D during the school year."

My dad places the screwdriver on the ground and picks himself off the floor. He grasps his cold beer and takes a large gulp. He overemphasizes the enjoyment he gets from the refreshment. "We don't got the money."

"Aw, come on, dad! Let's just save some time and skip the lesson. Just $10." The directness of my statement fires from my mouth like a missile.

"Ten dollars?!"

"It's just a few pennies."

"No, no, no. You have it backward, son. We don't save time and then spend pennies. Pennies are for saving and time is for spending. For example, we are spending time right now, *pero* I am going to go ahead and save my pennies." I must admit. He nailed it and I don't know how to effectively respond to him. So, I try humor.

"Can I interest you in a compromise? $9? But only if you act now!"

"Out! *¡Vete ahora!*" As I walk away I can hear him fumble around with the chair and mumbling to himself, "*¿Por qué me estás jodiendo? ¿Quieres dinero? Puedes besarme el culo…Y esta come pinga aquí…*"

My head is hanging low in defeat. A typical day-in-the-life of the *Wegotnomunie* family. Then I hear a pressured, soft voice. "Psst. Tommy. Here. Come here." Mom is hiding just behind the corner in the next room. Her hand reaches out and she gives me a wink. I look down. My palm is swallowed in the jaws of a wrinkled, but legal tender, pair of $5 bills. There is a conspiracy afoot in the home and the old man is only about 15 feet away. I am a co-conspirator so I might as well enjoy the fruits.

"Later, Dad. Love you!"

"This damn piece of *mierda*! *¿Cómo? ¡Repites!* Oh, yeah. Yeah. Have fun."

I kiss my mother on her forehead and I'm out the door.

4

THE BONFIRE

Jacob and I arrive together at Stoner's. The glow of the bonfire burning furiously can be seen on the other side of Stoner's house. He lived there with his adoptive mother, Christine. She was one of those "cool" mothers who didn't care what we did as long as we didn't wreck the place. I could see where Stoner got his devil-may-care attitude. Despite his name, he wasn't into drugs. The rest of the crew gave him that name in middle school because he talked much more slowly than the rest and always seemed relaxed. To me, Stoner was the most intelligent out of all of us. I had to look up to see Stoner's eyes and a brisk wind could make his body sway. Todd was what his family called him. He was also a bass guitar player—he loved jazz. His dream was to play damp clubs filled with cigarette smoke and spilled beer.

"I got to piss, you wanna help?" Jacob smirks.

"Nah. I'm good…I am going to head to the fire pit." Jacob reaches out like he is going to shake my hand. He can be so stupid sometimes. I swat his hand away and walk to the backyard.

I see Pierre and Kyra sitting in front of the fire. I can see just a small piece of a silhouette coming from the other side of the fire. I know it's Katrina. I must stay calm. This is potentially a big night. An evening when Katrina would lean her head against my shoulder. I would hold her hand. She tells me about her suffering. I tell her that everything is alright.

Kyra glares back towards me as I approach. She does not look happy. She is not next to Katrina, which is a bit weird, and she is throwing pieces of loose foliage into the fire. Her eyes glimmer in the waves of the flames and I can tell there are a few tears. I finally get up to where she is at. "What's up, Kyra bear-ah?"

Pierre greets me with a fist pump. Kyra shakes her head and motions over to where Katrina is sitting. About a quarter way around the fire, I get a better picture of the situation. My heart falls through my stomach and into my wobbling legs. Katrina is sitting with a big smile on her face. Her right arm encircles a quarter of the way around his arm. He's sitting there with his smug, foul face.

"Tom-o, what's up, bro?" I erupt mentally. I am not a "bro." I don't say it out loud.

Katrina sits up a little, "Hey, you. Grab a seat." I'd rather not, but what was I going to do? I act like something is preventing me from sitting closer to Katrina and I plop down next to Kyra. I look at Kyra and mouth out, "What the hell?"

She mouths back, "Dick." Kyra is so unassuming. I giggle under my breath.

The silent conversation continues, "I know, right?"

I don't even want to waste any time talking about Deron. The *perra* is a prick. A prick of the first order. He treats Katrina like trash—like rubbish that rolls up next to his foot. He cares only enough to pick it up briefly and then throws it in a trash can. I never knew what Katrina was thinking when she picked these jerks. If the guy was bad to her, she was attracted to him. I would treat her so much better. I do treat her better.

Jacob finally made his way to the fire and when he sees Deron he blurts out, "I thought you were history, dude?"

"Stop it, Jacob!" Katrina retorts, squinting her eyes in disapproval.

"We, uh, worked it out, bro. You know I can't stay away from my hot girl." Deron cups his hand on Katrina's opposite cheek and turns her head towards him, "Right, baby?" He forces a kiss. I want to replace her lips with my fist.

"Whatever, dude. Anybody got a beer or something?" Jacob is the one who likes to party.

Stoner who had been characteristically quiet chimes in, "Yeah, over there in the ice chest, under Pierre's ass."

Here we are. A sacred place. All of us together. And Deron. Pricklord himself.

The pleasure of the night is not completely lost. We finally loosen up and start joking around. The fire has subsided a little and the aura of red heat surrounds the charcoal. The evening is otherwise quiet. The sky is clear, and the stars are shining from horizon to horizon. I look up and notice Orion's belt.

"Orion is cool," I suggest.

"It's crazy the stars are so far away, yet we can see them." Pierre sets his beer down and tosses another log on the fire.

Stoner blows our minds away. "You know, that is light from millions of years ago. It takes that long to get to us. If there is another life out there, it will take them millions of years to see the light we are giving off tonight."

"Whoa, that's crazy, Stoner." Jacob, half-drunk, grabs his forehead in amazement.

"I don't think there is anything else out there." Deron

unwelcome-like enters the conversation. "I mean, wouldn't we know already?"

Stoner responds, "Perhaps. Perhaps. I don't think you can say that because we haven't seen them that they don't exist."

"Okay? I don't know, bro," Deron sarcastically responds. "I'm just worried about what is right here." He squeezes Katrina. She is swooning. I just want to punch him in the face or throw him in the fire.

I desperately want to change the subject. I am not sure how long I can listen to Deron's idiocy. What a prick. I finally dream up something to keep him quiet for a while. "Hey, what are you guys going to do after graduation? Pierre, you start."

PIERRE ST-LAPE. All Pierre wanted to do was become a famous chef. We rarely went to Pierre's house because the TV would inevitably end up showing some hapless wanna-be chef pouring tears over his rejected under-seasoned chicken. Pierre was a great cook for a high school kid. His parents had migrated from Haiti before he was born. Pierre frequently told us he was a spy for the Haitian government and the only reason he was hanging out with a bunch of mainlanders was to steal the secrets of the American teenager. This joke was his way of letting us know he identified with his Haitian heritage. However, our involvement with Pierre was his great taste in music. He could not find many other Haitians who liked punk and thrash metal. Nonetheless, it was behind the metal handle of a cheap pot where Pierre excelled. When he cooked, he nailed it every time! Still, within him was sadness. No matter how much food he cooked, there was always a famine. It followed him every day, everywhere. Pierre existed in a deep gulch where he couldn't find any external respect.

He worked for his uncle and no matter what he did, he was paid in insult and nitpicking. The pain was far below the surface because Pierre was otherwise all too eager to meet new people and his energy never waned when the spotlight finally came to him, however briefly.

"I HAVEN'T DECIDED EXACTLY YET. As long as I can cook, I will be okay. My uncle says he is going to let me prep cook when I graduate, but he says a lot of things. One day. One day, people will know my name." Pierre emphasizes that last line. He was hungry for something more than food.

Kyra jumped into the fray. "I am going to go get my A&P as soon as I can."

"What's that," Deron interjected.

"It's Airframe and Powerplant, it's basically an airplane mechanic."

Deron laughs. "Mechanic? You are a tomboy, aren't you?

I think to myself that Kyra is going to get up and murder him. "Why do I have to be a tomboy to work on airplanes?"

"Calm down. Don't get all worked up." Oh, oh, Kyra does not like to be mansplained. This prick just mansplained her. But I am proud of Kyra. She just continues.

"Any whatchasays, I haven't decided what school to go to but my aunt is a pilot for Melody Airlines and she said they need A&Ps all of the time."

"That is so hot," Stoner replies. He is looking in awe at Kyra. He's in love, too. However, he has no problem saying it. "That's why I love you, Kyra."

"I love you, too, Stones." Kyra usually follows that with an "as a friend" qualifier. I suppose she is trying to be sensitive to his feelings in front of everyone. "What are you going to do, Stones?"

"Oh, I don't know. I am not into the rat race sort of lifestyle. I guess I will go to some mutant species of college or government indoctrination program, but I am not worried about it."

"For crying out loud, Stoner!" I'm a bit indignant. I struggled to get a C; Stoner gave Bs away like nothing. "You could have straight As and do whatever you want. Why don't you just get the As and become a high-powered lawyer or something?"

"No, man. That's not me. Just because you have an A doesn't mean you know jack. I'm not going to worry about it. Things will work out. Besides, the law is Katrina's gig. Ain't that right?"

"I love that courtroom stuff!" Katrina started glowing. "I am taking my SAT again. I scored a 1550 the last time. I just need about 30 more points for Harvard."

"Harvard?" The pricklord interrupts again. "Isn't that where all of the really, really smart stuck-up people go? Are you sure Harvard is for you?" Katrina is visibly hurt and deflates her shoulders. "I'm just playing, baby. It was just a joke."

Kyra has had enough. "So, let me understand this: you think there is a certain place for a woman to be?"

"Wow! I didn't say that. You're so angry for a girl," a recoiling Deron says.

"Oh, no? I'm a tomboy because I want to work on airplanes and she is what, just a stupid girl or something? If she doesn't belong at Harvard, where does she belong? Barefoot in Deron's kitchen?"

Deron blushes. He really does not know what to say. Kyra was on her battle horse and hankering to rip someone's head off. The intensity was terrifying. In so many ways, Kyra is my heroine—if I were not so frightened of her.

Kyra was not the one to trifle with. She is a firecracker, a bomb with a timer set to one second. Her well-defined chin towered over most of the other girls. The emerald eyes with which she observed the world are mesmerizing and unique. Thin, muscular Kyra is probably the strongest and most daring of us all; however, she has her feminine pride. Getting under her skin is as simple as insinuating she had little femininity. Deron is discovering this trigger tonight.

I once witnessed Kyra give an epic beating to a stupid boy. He called her "tomboy," too, and then asked how big her balls were. Stupid boy. Before I knew it, she straddled her victim, her reaper's sickle ready to make the fatal blow. Stupid, stupid boy.

Stoner used his calm, steady voice to settle things back down a bit. "Okay. Okay. We have enough heat coming from this fire. Let's play a game or something."

Jacob did his best to break the tension, too, "Well, I am going to be a male stripper and I am going to wear assless underwear—that will be my signature thing. My stage name is Max Hang."

"There is something really wrong with you, man," Kyra blurts out in a repulsed shiver. It's effective. We certainly have forgotten about women mechanics and Ivy League institutions.

We are getting tired. It is almost three in the morning, and we smell like campfire smoke. In my mind, I'm thinking about all of our plans after high school. I realized nobody asked me what I was going to do. I can feel my heart pumping inside my chest, but I'm not sure why. Stoner yawns and pushes his arms into the air to stretch. Kyra is now sitting next to Katrina holding her. Deron is already asleep. My eyes scan around the bonfire once more and I suddenly feel compelled to express an impromptu, seemingly crazy idea. "Hey! When we graduate, we all should travel the world together for a year!"

"I'm in," Jacob lifts his head and gives me a thumbs up.

"That would be cool, Tommy." Stoner approves.

"I always wanted to see Korea," replies Kyra.

Jacob stares into the sky. "Korea? Who wants to go to Korea?"

"I do!"

Pierre claps his hands and clasps them together, "France! I want to go to the finest restaurant in Paris."

I am realizing we all have different places we want to see. I modify the fantasy to keep it alive. "You know what we should do? We should travel the world separately and at the end of the year meet somewhere."

Katrina finally joins us, "After I finish my time in Milan, where?"

"I don't know. How about…" I am a bit unsure. I pause and then say the first place that comes to mind, "Prague?" I shrug my shoulders.

"Prague? What the hell is in Prague?" Kyra is unsure, too.

"It just came to me. I am not sure why. Just…Prague."

"Works for me," Jacob confirms his agreement.

Stoner raises his hand to give Jacob a high five, "Yes! Prague sounds okay to me, too!"

"Any *whatchasays*, sure, Prague, what about you Kat?" Kyra concedes. Katrina just nods her head. I know she plans to go to Harvard and become a lawyer; however, I am hoping she is getting excited by this half-cocked idea.

"It's settled. When we graduate, we all travel where we want to go and we end up in Prague a year later."

Jacob waves his hands in the air, "Alright! Max Hang is going to Prague! Right after Amsterdam!"

Kyra throws a pinecone at Jacob. "You are so gross!"

I know that we are just talking. The truth is I am a bit excited at the idea of us having a grand adventure together after high school.

5

GRADUATION

Katrina looks amazing. Her makeup is perfect, not that she needs any makeup to be beautiful. She is all smiles. Her mother sits in a wheelchair in the front row, an oxygen machine accompanying her. It is a miracle she has made it to this day. Sitting next to her is twenty-one-year-old Anthony. I suspect he is after Katrina although Katrina says that they are only friends. Still, the jealousy rages. I put my arms around Katrina. "I am so glad your mother is here to see you walk. Your daddy would be so proud."

Her eyes swell and tears begin to form. "Stop, I am going to mess up my makeup." She carefully wipes under her eyes.

"You don't need makeup. You are the prettiest girl I know."

Katrina playfully slaps me. "Shut up! No, I'm not!" My dad used to tell me if a girl playfully slaps you and tells you to shut up, she likes you. I don't know. If she liked me, then why is Anthony sitting out there with his fake grin? "Thank you. You are so sweet."

"I still think you should go to Harvard."

"I am. I just have to wait a year or two. Anthony is

helping me with Mom, and I just need to make sure she is okay before I go, you know?" Her eyes cock off to the left and her shoulders tighten up. She wipes a few more tears. They keep trickling out like a leaking faucet.

"Promise me you will go be a lawyer."

She laughs. "Okay. I will."

"Good, because I plan on doing some really messed up things and I 'm going to need a smart lawyer to get me off the hook." Her smile widens.

"What's up, bitches!" Kyra lifts her graduation gown to keep it from dragging on the floor. "Oh, look at Clarissa Banks. She is so sexy. I might see what she is doing later tonight. Wink, wink." Kyra found a growing attraction for other women at the beginning of our senior year. She told me that she refuses to struggle with the idea. Her mantra has been, "I am what I am, and I do what I do." She is so synchronized with her feelings and not in the least bit afraid to see where they lead her.

"Isn't she dating Matt Stofer?"

"So? Who's cuter, me or Matt Stofer? Duh!" Behind her sarcasm, I could hear the bloodied sickle swishing through the air. I think I might always fear Kyra in some way.

"You are. No question."

"Glad you agree with me. Not that you have a choice." Bubble gum balloons out of her mouth and pops.

The teachers and administrators hurry us to get in line. We are about to walk out. All of us are in the same general area in line except Stoner and Pierre. They are "R" and "S," so they are far in the back. One of the teachers asks, "Hommel? Where is Hommel?" I have a good feeling he is hidden away somewhere getting a few last puffs of his THC vape. While Kyra is figuring out her feelings for girls, Jacob is figuring out his feelings for marijuana.

I yell out loudly, "Max! Calling Max to the stage!" The

sound of chairs hitting the hard floor suddenly echoes through the hallway. Jacob emerges smiling, his eyes like pink carnations. He high-fives me as he passes by. He is just in time. The music starts and we commence the slow waltz to our chairs.

The principal, Ms. Mathers, is proudly upright in her black gown receiving diplomas from Tommyhawk. The announcer is droning through names and then I hear, "Jacob Carter Hommel, blah, blah, blah, Katrina Annette Johnson, blah, blah, blah, Kyra Hillary Livingston, blah, blah, blah, Thomas Enrique Sotomayor Lopez…" I'm carefree walking toward the podium. I see Mr. Beady looking at me with those thin, immovable lips. I nod. He shakes his head. I shrug my shoulders and make a stressed, goofy smile. He shakes his head. I get back to my seat and open my diploma. The paper is baby blue, like our school colors. It's beautiful. I look over at Katrina and Kyra. Smiles. "Blah, blah, blah, Todd Roberts, blah, blah, blah, Pierre Michael Saint-Lape, blah, blah, blah." The final name is called, and we stand and hug each other. Now I want time to be as slow as physics will allow. Before I know it, we are taking pictures—lots of pictures. We are making promises to see each other frequently. Some of us are crying, others are about to cry.

Kyra's dad comes over and tells her they have a restaurant reservation. They need to leave. She hugs me. She walks away.

Pierre is the next to depart. He is going straight to work. He walks away.

Stoner hugs me. "Don't let them change you, Tommy."

"Change me? Who?"

"Them."

"Who the hell is 'them?'" I'm almost certain what he is talking about, but I like to listen to him carry on. He points his finger at me like a big brother warning the younger, twirls, and heads for the exit. He walks away.

"Dude, I gotta get out of here. My buzz is wearing off and I'm stressing out a little bit." Jacob hugs me. He walks away.

Finally, it is time to say goodbye to Katrina. Anthony pushes Katrina's mom up beside us. "Can you believe it? Yay! I am a graduate." I go to hug Katrina again. Anthony steps into my line of sight and intercepts her arms. I drop my arms and turn away to give my attention to Katrina's mom.

"Hey, Ms. Edinburgh, I bet you are super proud right now."

The rush of oxygen pushing into her nostrils is audible. They have increased her dosage. "Yes, yes. I'm so proud of my Katrina. I knew she could do it! Anthony and I are taking her to celebrate."

Anthony rests his arm on Katrina's shoulders like a dog pissing on a fire hydrant marking its territory and begins to usher her away. Katrina turns her head back and with her gorgeous smile yells, "Congrats, Tommy! I love you!" That crushing sound is my heart. Ms. Edinburgh struggles to keep up. Once they are clearly out of hugging distance, the conniving Anthony takes control of the wheelchair again. They walk away.

My parents finally find me in the crowd. "Dad, what fancy restaurant are you taking me to for graduation?"

"How does a burger from Burger Shack sound?" He is so cheap.

My mother twists her body around like a slingshot and lands an elbow into my dad's rib. "Stop it! We are going to go wherever you want, son. Your dad will just have to deal with it." Dad shrugs his shoulders and smiles. We walk away.

6

PAPA D

F*our years later.*

"TOMMY, can you come over here and help Ms. Hernandez load up her truck?"

"Sure thing, Papa D." I place a large sheet of plywood that I am carrying on the floor. "Good afternoon, Ms. Hernandez, what did we get today?"

Papa D points to a pile of floor tile planks. "She got 20 linear feet of that 8 x 24 white plank ceramic."

"Oh, nice choice! You nailed it, Ms. Hernandez. This should only take a few minutes." I load the tile carefully into a candy-red pickup truck.

I have been working for Papa D since I was a sophomore in high school. Originally, I only worked during the summers. After I graduated the work became full-time. The job isn't too bad. It's a living. Papa D is a friend of the family, and he is a fair man. Last Spring, he promoted me to Assistant Manager. The pay is sufficient—enough to afford a car and a small apartment on the outskirts of town. I do not spend my money on much—a trait I picked up from Dad. However, I do at times get bored.

A slightly ducked-footed and rotund man, Papa D is an old friend of the family and a frequent tres leches consumer. A local boy now all grown up and living in the same home he experienced childhood. He lived away for a while. A military veteran. I think it was the Navy. They sent him to Asia where he met his wife, Yura. He was 19, she was 18. He is now 62 and she, as he insists, is "still 18." I don't even know what his real name is—Domingo, Dominic, or something like that. I have called him Papa D since I was born. When he returned from the service, he opened up the flooring store. His father was the mayor some time ago and his uncle was a police officer. My mother tells me she used to play over at Papa D's house with his younger cousin Nina. When my dad first met my mother, it was Papa D who set them up. The day my father proposed to my mother, Papa D was the first to know. Always the generous gentleman, he hired me on as a part-time helper for more than minimum wage.

SINCE WE GRADUATED the gang has not kept in touch the way I would have wanted. In fact, they have drifted away from me. Sure, there were a few times within the first year we got together. Now, we follow each other on Oratr, the latest in the social media experience. Kyra, Pierre, and Stoner are doing okay. Jacob is a mess. I see him around town from time to time. I think he may be living on the streets. I say hello, but he is not the same. Katrina ended up marrying that Anthony guy. I understand he is just like her stepfather. He doesn't treat her well and I heard the neighbors called the cops on them a few times because of the fighting. I still have an overwhelming infatuation for her. She is still beautiful and when she replies to my messages, I get all giddy. We have been out of high school for years and I still have fantasies about her. Of course, I have had a few girlfriends. They never match up to Katrina—at least not in my mind—and I loose interest.

"I am going to leave a little early today. My grandson has a baseball game. Can you close up?"

"Of course, Papa D. No problem." He collects the large bulk of metal that is his keys and turns his computer off. He departs out the heavy glass door and the shop is all mine.

I have a few closing chores I need to do. I sit down behind my desk to take in a few minutes of quiet. On my desk is a picture of Jacob, Kyra, Katrina, Pierre, Stoner and me together in our graduation gowns. Dust has collected on the frame. I am thinking why I can't move on when they have. I want to go back to high school just so I can hang out with them around a bonfire. On the corner of a desk is a worn map of Europe. There is a big red circle around London. Then a thin line goes through Paris and towards the west of France. I have put a star next to a town called Auray. The reason why is a mystery to me. Perhaps, I simply liked the way the town name sounded. The fading line then heads into Switzerland, Germany, Austria, and Poland. The end of the trail is almost completely unreadable. I am sure I know where it ends: Prague. The colors are disappearing as the hue of the world seems to gray in my dismal daydream. I take a deep, self-soothing breath. I return to closing the store and I go home.

7

JACOB

I'm fast asleep at about six in the morning. My phone vibrates on my cluttered nightstand. Who in the hell is calling me at this hour? The face of the phone says "Momma." I am not fully awake yet, but the name registers. I scramble to grab the phone. It falls to the floor, and it is still shaking furiously. Finally, I get a tepid grip on it and answer the call.

"Mom? What's going on? Is dad okay?"

"Hey, honey. Your dad's fine. He is snoring away in the bedroom." I am now coming to shallow consciousness and my basic faculties are with me.

"Okay. You wouldn't call me this early unless something was wrong, so spill it."

"I'm sorry, son. It's Jacob."

"Jacob, yeah, I just saw him a couple of weeks ago. What did he do?"

"He's gone."

"Gone? What do ya mean 'gone?'" I am genuinely confused.

"He died, Tommy. Last night."

Sickness surges inside my stomach. I can sense the spin of the earth. I slide back down into a supine position holding the phone to my ear. "Wait. He's dead? How do you know?"

"I heard it from Dr. Lee, my boss. He was leaving after doing rounds at the neonatal unit. He said he went through trauma on his way out and heard some say Jacob's name. I used to talk about you kids at the office, so he recognized it."

The room becomes soundless, and my mother's voice is incoherent. A moment ago I could clearly interpret the familiar rhythm of her speech, the wide sweeps of her inflection. There is an involuntary disconnection in my heart causing my body's senses to dull. Then a sickness fills my gut and pours sorrow into my stomach. Time is passing in a moment in which I am existing stationary. Jacob, the obnoxious, heart-full-of-love soul has become the companion of angels. A part of me has departed from the living. The phone begins to drop from my ear like a drunk's drool. The sensation brings me back.

"Why? Why did he die?"

My mother understands. She is always the empath and perceives I am seeking more explanation than the cause of his death. "Son, life is full of events without a reason other than what God knows. Jacobs was a good young man. I liked him. I really did. His demons simply got the best of him."

"It's not fair! He was dealt such a crappy deal."

"Yes."

My own voice is getting louder, and my pace is faster. "He was kind but this stupid world spit on him; Left him with nothing and then, and then," I have to pause to bring my quivering lips to rest, "Jesus…why is he gone, Mom?"

There is a gap in the conversation. There is silence.

"Tommy?"

"I'm here."

"I can't imagine what you feel right now, but as a mother,

this is why I want you to protect yourself in this life. It's fragile."

"I will, Mom, I will. What killed him?"

"Deep internal pain that drove him to turn to drugs to cover that pain. He overdosed. He overdosed on Fentanyl." I knew what took his life before she told me. "I know this is a lot to take in."

"Yeah. I hope his mother was the first thing he saw when he passed." The thought hits me. I begin to let my emotions show.

"Why don't you call Papa D and take the day off?"

I appreciate my mother's suggestion. Still, I need to get my mind off things. We exchange a few more words and the worst phone call I have ever had in my life unceremoniously ends, just like Jacob's life.

8

PESTILENCE

There is no way I am going back to sleep, so I take a shower and spend a few minutes on Oratr to see if anyone is talking about Jacob. Nobody. It just happened. The news has not escaped the police and coroner's reports yet. I begin to type out words ferociously, but I find them much too sad. I want to celebrate Jacob. I delete what I have so far.

I try again. Too happy. Delete.

A third attempt. Stupid. Delete. I get up from the chair and mope into the kitchen.

Bzzz. Bzzz.

New post from Todd Robertson on Oratr.

RIP Jacob Hommel. Died last night.

A PERFECT MESSAGE. I guess the word is out now.

Bzzz. Bzzz.

New response from Kyra Livingston on Oratr.
Oh, no! Wut happd?

Bzzz. Bzzz.
New response from Todd Robertson on Oratr.
Overdose.

Bzzz. Bzzz.
New response from Kyra Livingston on Oratr.
This sad.

Bzzz. Bzzz.
New response from Pierre Saint-Lape on Oratr.
O Bondye! What did he do? Are you sure?

Bzzz. Bzzz.
New response from Todd Robertson on Oratr.
Yes. The guy he was shooting up with was my cousin's friend. He almost died, too. They said they gave them like 5 of those things that are for overdoses. The guy made it. Jacob didn't.

Bzzz. Bzzz.
New response from Pierre Saint-Lape on Oratr.
I always was worried when he was getting stoned in HS.

I AM WATCHING these messages multiply like a starving virus. Paralyzed. I wanted to celebrate his life, but they are talking about the drugs. I should jump in.

. . .

Bzzz. Bzzz.

New response from Kyra Livingston on Oratr.

Yeah. Me 2. I kinda felt this would happn.

This isn't the way to remember him. I need to say something now! My thumbs are frantically pounding the screen. I keep misspelling words. *"Reid?" No, trust*! *"Frowns?" No, friend*! This damn piece of *mierda*! Come on!

Bzzz. Bzzz.

Bzzz. Bzzz.

Bzzz. Bzzz.

DAMN IT! The phone launches from my hand and collides with the farthest wall away from me. My fingertips oscillate in tiny random circles and my pores bleed sweat into my shirt. The hell with this! I am feeling anger start to swoop in and grip me; powerful talons squeezing together the chambers of my heart. Suffocating. Infuriating. Demoralizing.

9

LEVIATHAN

Papa D went into the store early in the morning, so he met me as I entered. A sheet of tile in his hands he immediately stops and looks at me as if he is surprised. He sips his coffee and then speaks. "What are you doing here?"

"It's eight-thirty, Papa D. I'm on the schedule for today."

"I know that! I made the schedule. I heard what happened. You should take the day off." My mother had obviously called him and offered her opinion.

"Thanks. Honestly, I need to keep my mind busy today. I'm fine to work."

"Are you sure?"

"Yes." The response is immediate and automatic. The words leaves my mouth before I even think about his question. I'm not sure. Not sure in the least. Unsure.

"Okay. I can respect that. Why don't you work in the staging area today? You can get some fresh air and a bit of manual labor."

"Yeah, sure, Papa D." I am in such a daze that I walk past him guessing the placement of the next step.

A couple of hours go by and there is only light foot traffic in the store. Papa D comes to the staging area and brings me some water. He is always drinking water. "Do you want to talk about it?"

"I'm not sure. I still can't believe he's gone."

"Sure. Sure. It's going to take time."

"The funny thing is that I don't even know why I am taking this so hard. I mean, we were friends and we sometimes talked with each other, but it is not like we hung out all of the time."

Papa D sips his water. "Yep." He is always thirsty.

"I don't know if it is because I'm really shocked or if it is something else. I know I am going to miss that part of my life, but it still doesn't make much sense, you know?"

"Yep."

I crack a smile and let a short burst of laughter slip out. "If I didn't know you better, I'd say you have an opinion about this situation." I take a sip of water to mirror Papa D.

"Well, I can't say for sure, of course, but I have been around a few years, and I have known you for a while."

"Yep."

"Do you remember a few years ago when we had old Leviathan?"

"The dog?"

"Yes. The dog. Do you remember how upset you got when I told you I had to put him down?"

I am puzzled. "Uh, yeah, I guess."

"Do you remember how you walked around here like if he was your dog? You talked about him for months. Remember?"

I am thinking really hard right now trying to imagine that time. "I remember being a little sad, yes."

"It's not that you talked about Levi, it's how you talked about the time when Levi was here. You saw it as a major change in your world. You actually said that the 'world changes, but I am doing the same things.' Remember that?"

"Vaguely."

"Tommy, you hold on to the past. You are afraid to take chances. Don't take this the wrong way: Son, you can't handle change very well. Your friend was a change that affected your life back to high school. Understand?"

My back curls, my shoulders slump forward, and my head dips. I have no idea what he is talking about, though his sincerity leads me to believe he knows something. I take another sip of water. I'm stalling. I'm thinking of denying it. No, that's stupid. How about if I say…nah, equally dumb. Maybe denial is the way to go.

"You're doing it now." Papa D smirks at me and takes another sip of his water. "You can't make up your mind and your brain is turning like a pinwheel."

"Uh, well, um. I, uh." Crap. He's nailing it.

"Okay. Let me ask you a question. When you and your friends were in school, what is the thing you remember the most?"

I sip my water once more. "Uh, I suppose hanging out; going to movies; talking to each other…"

"No, no, no," he interrupts me. "I am not talking about general things you did. If you were to describe you and your friends and how you all saw the world, what would you say?"

"I don't know." I'm being honest. "I just remember that everybody wanted to do something with their lives."

"And, what about you?"

The question causes my brain to seize. I am thinking but no answer comes to mind. I can remember what Pierre wanted to do; Katrina; Kyra; Stoner; even Jacob. I cannot think about what I wanted to do. I am realizing now that I did not think about it too much. "I really don't know, Papa D.

I guess I figured I would just work here until things worked out."

"Hmmm. Your plan was to take high school with you? I mean you probably thought you and your friends would stay close and continue to do what you did while in school. Am I on track?"

He is eerily on point! I did believe we would stay close. I did believe we would keep watching movies and hanging out at Stoner's. I still believe that Katrina is going to come to her senses and realize I'm the one for her. She's married. She has a kid on the way. Everyone changed except me. I need another sip of water.

"Think about it, kid. I have faith that you will figure it out. What did Tommy want to do in life?" Papa D takes a larger gulp of water. "There cannot be peace until you are able to throw the past into the abyss." He wipes his mouth and excuses himself because the lunchtime shoppers are starting to arrive.

My dad used to say, "It's better to know what today brings than to speculate about tomorrow because today is much cheaper than tomorrow." I suppose that advice was taken to heart. I never envisioned a tomorrow: spending my time and saving my pennies with my eyes focused on my feet.

10

CONSPIRACY

Every day I get up on the same bed I've had since middle school. The materials of the bed are broken down from the decade of heat and sweat. The lumps are uneven. Still, I never once considered replacing it. Next to the bed on the nightstand is a rock. Nothing special about this rock. It's a rock. I got it when mom took me to the river at the state park. To be honest, I am not sure why I picked that rock or any rock. Nonetheless, every time I look at it, I remember the river. The reflection of the sun off the ripples on the water and the gently swaying trees. The rocks covered the shoreline like a blanket and they tucked neatly under the water. I suppose it was a moment I wanted to keep with me so I left it with a memento.

The alarm is ringing and I toss in that familiar bed. My hand explores the nightstand top stumbling across the river rock, my phone, a few miscellaneous items and I'm stabbing blindly with my fingers. Finally, I locate the snooze button. How many times have I reached for that button? Perhaps a thousand instances and I still can't find it with precision. The thought frightens me. I control this entire environment, yet there is randomness every day. The shock of fear finishes the job of waking me up. I lift my head, turn off the alarm completely, and then make my way into the bathroom. The day's routine has begun. It's 7:32 AM and a toothbrush is scraping my gums.

Papa D is at the store and I am about five minutes late. "Nice for you to join us today." The sarcasm is spread thickly.

"I know, I know." I place my keys down on my desk. "I just got a little behind. It won't happen again."

He sips his coffee and places it down on his desk. Papa D smirks and playfully responds, "Oh, I have a feeling it won't." He walks away from me and the meaning of his words misses their mark. He can be a touch cranky before his second cup.

I see on the board there are several orders so I walk out to the warehouse. A figure stands in front of me bent over moving around some tiles. I do not recognize him at all. The cheap cologne is not familiar and it's strong and putrid. "Can I help you?" My voice does not hide my indignation well. "Customers shouldn't be in this area, sir." The young guy stands up and turns to me with a puzzled look. His cologne is burning the hair out of my nostrils. On his hands are a pair of thick leather gloves and his boots are fit for a construction worker. These blue-collared guys always think they know about everything and initially disregard my assistance. "Sir, if you return to the storeroom, we can talk about what you need."

"Ah, Tommy, I see you have met Steven."

Steven? Who in the hell is Steven? Why is Steven in the warehouse rummaging through expensive titles? I'm confused. "Uh, Steven? Nice to meet you, Tommy. Papa D?" I apologetically glance towards Steven. "No offense Steven, but, Papa D, why is Steven in the warehouse?"

"He works here."

Despite my best attempts, I cannot process why Steven now works with us. Papa D didn't mention a thing. I don't like it. "Works here? Since when?"

"Since I hired him, numbskull." That smirk. This situation must be some kind of joke. "What's the matter, the owner of the company can't hire workers?"

"Of course, you can. I am just a bit confused. I didn't know you were looking for additional help."

"Additional? Hell no! I can't afford that." Papa D's belly is jiggling like Santa Claus'. He is moving like a holiday icon and I am standing in complete confusion. "Let's go talk in the office, Tommy." He giggles some more.

We enter the office and Papa D closes the door behind him. "I don't understand. If you can't afford more help, then why did you hire someone else to help?"

"Do you remember our discussion a few weeks ago?" He reclines in his beat-up office chair.

"What discussion?"

"The one about Jacob, high school, and all the other stuff."

I remember, but I try to stall for time. "I mean, I remember we had some discussion about dealing with Jacob's passing."

Papa D leans forward and motions toward the chair next to his desk. This seat is where he sits his toughest customers. Many times, I have seen him close a deal that I thought was long lost. "Sit for a moment, Tommy." I do. "You have had some time. What did you come up with?"

He knows I remember but I play it dumb a little bit longer. "Come up with? For what?"

"C'mon, Tommy. Tommy is sitting in his room. It's his sophomore or junior or senior year of high school. He is thinking about graduation. What does he want to do?"

I am uncomfortable. Very uncomfortable. Perhaps a snippet scared. "I, I, don't know."

"Okay. What is on Tommy's walls? What pictures line his wall?"

"I don't know. I think I had some band posters. A few other pictures of some other stuff."

"What are those pictures of?" Papa D is an effective investigator.

"Uh, I think I had a picture of the Eiffel Tower. I also had a picture of some castle in Germany or something."

"So, you have pictures of places far away?"

"I guess so. Mom always used to talk about places she wanted to go, so I suppose I found a few places of interest to me."

"Bingo!" Papa D slams his fist on the desk. "Is it safe to say that you wanted to travel?"

"Yeah. Sure."

Papa D leans back in his creaking chair. "What if I told you that based on everything I know about you, you wanted to travel–as your mother wanted to do–and in your mind, you somehow thought all of your friends wanted to go, as well? Am I close?"

"Papa D, I, um, that was just high school." The wheels are spinning in my head. He nailed it again. I pause. I finally admit, "Okay, yes. We made a pact that we would travel for a year and meet somewhere after–but I know that was just talking."

The phone rings. Papa D holds up his finger to put the conversation on hold. I'm glad. I need a few moments to get my mind straight. All comfort has left me. Steven is in the warehouse doing who knows what and Papa D is interrogating me like some career criminal. He answers the phone. "Yes. I am talking to him right now." He listens to the person on the other side. "So far, so good. About what I expected. We are getting to it now." I can barely hear the other voice on the phone. It's a woman and she sounds familiar. Leaning in closer, Papa D's eyes stop me. I cannot hear enough to make it out. "Of course, no problem. It needs to be done. Okay, love you, too, Maria!" Maria? My mother?

"Was that my mother?"

"Yep."

"What were you talking about?"

Papa D's smirk turns into a wide, nervous smile. "Your mother and I had a long talk about two weeks ago." Papa D and my mother talking with one another is nothing new. They have been essentially family for years. I know the subject of discussion is obviously something much different. "We think you are too much like your dad." He bursts out laughing. "He is the most frugal person I know. He wouldn't spend money unless he is forced."

"Yeah. That's true. But what does that have to do with me?"

"Your dad, as much of a miser he is, has an outlet. He spends other people's money so he can get rid of that urge with the family's money." The well-known cliche appears above the ends of my hair. "You on the other hand, you're stuck."

I interrupt Papa D. "I'm not stuck. I am saving my pennies, that's all."

Papa D almost falls over in laughter. "You sound exactly like your dad!" He finally gains a little composure and wipes a few genuine tears from his eyes. "Look, the bottom line is that we think it is best if you take that time you had put aside back in high school. Put it in action. Go. Travel. Experience something new."

The situation fully makes sense now. "So, that is where Steven comes in."

"Forget about Steven. How much money have you saved up now?"

After I pay my bills and catch a movie or two, I have been

saving about 30% of my check since I have worked for Papa D. "Not much. I have about $10,000 in my retirement account and about $27,000 in the bank."

"Good lord, boy! You have more cash than I do. You still play guitar?"

"Yep."

"So, you can make money while you travel, too." He sees the confused look on my face. "You have more than enough to travel, and you can make a few dollars here and there playing your guitar on the street. Very common in Europe. You can also work at a hostel in exchange for boarding."

"You can?"

"Yes! You need to go on that trip." I see what Papa D is doing. He is selling me this idea. This process is exactly what he does with his customers. He starts to get more excited until the customer is excited, too. I am not going to fall for it. "The sooner you do this the better. This is really exciting news!"

"News? Whoa, whoa, Papa D. There's no news." I laugh out loud. "I am not falling for one of your sales voodoo spells!"

"Oh, you're not?"

"No, sir."

"Are you sure?"

"Yep. Nice try, though."

"I see. You're fired."

My laughter stops. "I'm what?"

"Fired. You're fired. Effective immediately."

"But—but I didn't do anything. Why are you firing me?"

"Hmm. That is not the way I see it. Weren't you late today?"

"Oh, come on, Papa..."

"I am firing you for excessive tardiness."

"Excessive?"

"And insubordination."

"Insubordination?"

"Yes, insubordination; not recommended for rehire for the next 5 to 10 years." He twists his body around to get to the other side of the desk. He spins back around holding a piece of paper. "I like you too much, so you're fired. Here is your last paycheck. Here is your severance. And I talked to Harold Brooks. He is going to let you out of your lease at the end of this month for no charge–he owed me a favor." The severance check is 5,000 dollars. Papa D is the best.

"I don't know what to say. Thank you."

"Good. Now, clear out your desk and get out of here." Papa D stands up and opens the door to the warehouse. As he walks through the corridor he yells back, "See you this weekend at your parent's house."

11

THE FIRST DOLLAR

I have not even left yet, and my pennies are being spent in haste.

I AM LEAVING QUICKLY, so, expedited passport, $100; Vaccinations, $150; a quality backpack to live out of for a year, $200; 110v-220v converter that mom says I need, $30; One-way Ticket to London, $500!

MY ANXIETY IS ALREADY at a fever pitch. I have not seen one ancient statue. I have not had one morsel of a French baguette in my mouth. I have not felt the walls of a single castle. Yet, I have spent a thousand dollars. The voice of my father brightly echoes through the crevices in my brain: "...what are you doing? *Wegotnomunie* for that *mierda*!" The vibrations are rattling my ears causing my nose to itch.

In fact, he told me, "*Yougotnomunie* for all of that *mierda*." His face was deadpan and his eyes darker than usual. He took a sip of his beer, and I politely reminded him I was not using his money. He giggled, keeping the beer securely pressed against his lips. A big gulp and he pushed his open palm out into the air. "Exactly, you damn fool. You're spending your own money! *¡Coño!* Haven't I taught you a thing? Spend other people's money."

"Ok. Can I get some of yours?"

"Hell no!" He placed his arms around me and pulled me tightly into his chest. It took me a few moments to process what he was saying. I finally figured out he was joking—at least partly. My nostrils captured the aroma of chicharrónes and beer. "Learn everything you can, son. If you are going to spend the money, do it boldly." I was still in disbelief. He had never said anything like that to me. However, the sentiment could not undo two decades of training. I wanted to renege. I wanted to cancel the trip and go back to work.

My internal moralizer spoke to me in the form of Papa D's voice. The money was nothing but a convenient excuse to cover up my self-doubts. I was facing the manifestation of self-doubt in financial terms.

The immersive baptism of the fellowship of the "cha-ching" as Stoner would say—had begun with a deep burning sting. He used to call me *Pooruman*. This nickname is his attempt at a humorous description of my thriftiness based on an evil wizard from his fantasy books. Every time I would reconsider my previous promise to spend money, he would say, "Come down off the tower, *Pooruman*, and pitch in!" I suppose the first dollar is the hardest.

12

BAGGAGE CLAIM

"Folks, we are about 20 minutes from touchdown at London's Heathrow airport. Winds are calm out of the north east and the temperature on the ground is 54 degrees, that's about 12 degrees Celsius. Cloudy. Overcast with some light rain. I will be turning on the fasten seatbelt sign for the remainder of the flight. It was our pleasure to get you here safely. Let us be the first to welcome you to London, England."

I AM STANDING in line waiting for my backpack to appear on a large metal conveyor belt. I slept the entire flight, yet I'm still tired. I suppose I'm a little grouchy, but more so, I'm nervous. What am I doing here? Everyone speaks some sort of English, but I can hardly understand many of them. I have had to use the bathroom since I landed. I have not seen the first one since the airplane. Now, it is getting critical as my bladder is at full capacity.

"Excuse me."

A polite gentleman fitted with a long coat and a perfectly

knotted tie turns to see who is asking for his attention, "Good morning, mate. What do you need?"

"Do you know where the closest bathroom is?"

"Sure. It is right over there." His pointing finger raises in the air and indicates some location in the far-off distance.

"On the other side of that wall?"

"No, right there. Before the wall?" He looks somewhat perplexed, gazing at me with a confused expression.

"Uh, I am sorry. I don't see the bathroom."

"It's right there. See the yellow sign?"

"No, sir. I just see the one that says 'WC.'"

The gentleman is shaking his head. "First time to the U.K., mate?"

"Yes." I am laughing nervously.

"Here we say, 'water closet.' WC for short. That's what you Yanks call the restroom." He smiles.

A light bulb flickers and then turns on! I do my best to dim it to hide the surge of embarrassment. "Oh." I had passed at least five of these on the way to baggage claim. This could be a very long trip. I'm already culturally lost in a country where I supposedly know the language. What do they call a kitchen? Heat Room?

13

UNPLANNED ADVENTURE

"Welcome to Farnham!" Napping passengers are waking after a several-hour bus trip. Ten seats back from the door and I have to tighten my collar with my hand. The chill makes me wag like a wet dog. The station is much smaller than I imagined. The mix of stone and modern glass is beautiful, but I was expecting something much bigger. "Mind your step," the bus driver is politely reminding every disembarking person.

I have been in England for three weeks now. London was incredible. Most memorable for me was areas around the Thames River. I remember looking at some of these places on the Internet. Big Ben. Parliament. The Tower of London. Awe slapped me relentlessly as if I needed to wake from a fairy-tale dream. The pounding of boots onto the pavement surrounding Buckingham Palace was deafening. A tourist even caught the ire of one of the guards because she was nearly hugging him. I have no idea what he yelled—the accents still confound me—but we all jumped into the air. She fled like a wounded cat.

Each night is lonely though. I hate the time just before I fall asleep. My mind cannot escape the misery of Jacob's death and my heart cannot heal the wounds torn in Katrina's wake. This many weeks into my trip I had hoped these pains would lessen; however, I feel as if they are getting worse. They are not feelings in the normal sense. They are parasitic emotions as if they are not even my own. In the worst moments, the richness of the culture around me becomes dull and grayscale. My stomach churns like a witch's cauldron and the blood in my veins is cursed with a spell of lethargy. A few nights ago, I cried. It was brief and intense. During the day I am okay, I guess. Occasionally, my thoughts turn to day terrors, but the nights are certainly more fertile times for fright.

Four days ago, I decided that I would move on from jolly Ole England and start heading south. Before I did, I wanted to see another part of the country. Another American visitor staying at the same hostel told me he enjoyed Fareham. Now, he was a happy man. Slender, young, and scared of nothing save running out of time. His speech bounced like a rock skimming a lake's surface. His hands flailed when he got into a story. The pupils of his hazel-green eyes dilated frequently as he relived the adventure. He told me the best adventures were unplanned.

We met during breakfast, and he said he had been backpacking England and Scotland for several months. He kept a scrapbook of different small items like flowers and weeds. On his phone, he wrote in a diary and had at least a thousand pictures documenting his journey. Paul, that is his name, is electric. He brought me the furthest from my internal conflict so far. What can I say? He inspired me. I decided that I would open my Oratr account to the world and log everything I did. In fact, I made him the star of my very first post! He is also my first new follower.

We hung out for a day or two. He had seen most of what I wanted to see, but he was gracious and offered to be a tour guide of sorts. Nonetheless, I wanted to head to France and spend a month or two exploring. So, we said our goodbyes and I took him up on his recommendation for Fareham. My ticket was purchased, and I boarded the bus.

"MIND YOUR STEP, sir. Welcome to Farnham."

"Thank y— Farnham?"

"Yes, sir, Farnham."

"I thought we were going to Fareham!"

"No, sir, I am afraid we don't go to Fareham on this bus."

"Well, how far away is Fareham."

"Fareham is about 40 miles that way. This is Farnham." He keeps one foot on the steps and leans back to point his gloved finger straight off the front of the bus.

"Farnham? But I wanted to go to Fareham."

"Yes, sir. This is Farnham."

My bones are turning to mush as the weight of my backpack bears down on me. One last step off the bus and I walk to the counter. A pleasant woman greets me warmly and immediately can see the defeat on my face.

"Good afternoon, sir. How may I be of assistance today?"

"This is Farnham." I barely apply volume above a whisper. "I thought I was going to Fareham."

"Oh, dear." Her head tilts to read what is written on my ticket. "Yes, you are at the right place for the ticket. And you told the agent Fareham?"

Self-doubt is all I feel. The same conversation is replaying in my head on a loop. Each time the dialogue is different every time.

I said Fareham.

No, I said Farnham.

No, no, I didn't say anything at all because I pointed at the schedule.

The agent said Fareham.

Wait, maybe I did say something. "I honestly do not know what I did. I'm so sorry."

"No need to apologize, sir. I have a rather poor report for you, however. Unfortunately, no bus takes you directly to Fareham from here today. You will have to board a later carriage back to London, I'm afraid."

She is looking at me with a what-would-you-like-to-do face. She has been kind and patient, but I can sense several other people behind me. She can probably solve their problems. I collect the items placed down on the counter, thank her, and I'm walking towards a bench.

A half day behind me Steven is comfortable doing my old job and Papa D is giving him snarky remarks. Dad is at work spending other people's money. Mom is sitting on a cold doctor's office chair making appointments for sickly patients that are nestled in blankets in their own beds. Katrina is probably thinking about the mistakes she made. I cannot imagine what her no-good-loser-of-a-husband is doing. Hopefully, he isn't drunk and laying his cowardly fingers on her. Kyra is probably still thinking about how she would bury the body. I'm not sure how much they talk anymore. They certainly do not talk to me as much. Every year less and less. Maybe Papa D was right. I always thought we were going to be close. They have all moved on to something else and I am here in England getting on the wrong buses.

A ray of the sun is peeking through the dark-edged cotton balls in the sky. The heat is nice. Is England always this dreary? I just feel sad. Yet that sunlight has an effect. A full beam is landing on the ground. There is something about the hopefulness of light-piercing through sad sogginess. The bus does not leave out of here for some time so I might as well tour Farnham—or wherever the hell I am—take some pictures, put on a faux-happy mask, and update my Oratr account. I have four additional followers now. At least they are being entertained.

14

PARISIAN HOSPITALITY

"*Avez-vous de la monnaie?*" A man in tattered clothing stumbles to get in front of me. His arm is outstretched, and he is showing me his open palm.

"I'm sorry. I don't know what you are saying."

"Ah! You are American, no?" The muscles in his face relax and a friendly smile appears.

"Yes...uh...*oui!* Yes. American."

"*Bienvenue à Paris!* Welcome to Paris, my friend." Now both of his arms are stretched out in a showing of hospitality. "Do you know your way around the city?"

"No." I laugh nervously. "I just arrived from London."

The dinginess of the subway system in Paris surprises me. There are more beggars than in London and in certain corners, the caustic smell of urine lingers. Yet, the sounds of the French tongue echo through the concrete grotto. A nasally flowing river of audible indulgence. So romantic. So beautiful. Absolutely unintelligible to me. I'm fortunate to have made the acquaintance of an English speaker so quickly. Strangely, I understand him better than I did most of the English.

"Please. Let me help you. I know this city well."

I'm not opposed to removing the weight from my back for a few moments, so I set my backpack on the ground next to me. I produce a pocket map and the name of the hostel I am supposed to stay at for the week. "The directions say that the hostel is close to the Lourmel station?"

"Ah, yes. This is the number 8 train—towards Balard. You will have to change trains a couple of times, but no problem." I am relieved to have local knowledge of the area. He must explain it to me several times; however, I eventually feel confident enough to navigate the Parisian underground to my destination.

"Are all of the French people this nice?"

"French? No. Parisians, yes."

"There is a difference? I did not know that." His directness is gaining my confidence quickly. My attention is completely on him.

"But of course! Paris is romantic and cultured. Other places in France are good, too. Sadly, there are also those areas where they are unnecessarily rude—and maybe sneaky."

"*Merci!* Do you mind if I take a picture of you for my travel log? I take a step towards him.

A short hesitation and then he agrees. "Stay right there, I will come to you, my friend." He places dark sunglasses on his face and exaggerates a smile. The picture is snapped, and he hastily turns away.

"Goodbye, my friend!" I am a little disappointed he is walking away. He raises his hand and waves. "What is your name?" The desperation is clearly sounding through the tunnels.

"Jacques." His voice is fading. Soon another figure joins him as they disappear behind a concrete wall. My experience is memorialized in a post in Oratr.

I pick up my backpack and drop it on my fatigued shoulders. There is a small store a few yards away, so I slowly slither my way towards it. The conversation has left me hungry and the aroma seeping out of the store is charming me like a piper.

The man working behind the counter has the decades etched into his skin. Thick lenses are held in thin frames and most of his head reflects the store lights.

"Bonjour, monsieur!"

"Bonjour. Do you speak English?"

"Anglais? Non, c'est la France. Nous parlons français!" I have no idea what he is saying, but I know exactly what he is saying. His head is twisting left to right, and he is throwing his hands into the air. If I were forced to translate, I would say he refused to speak to me in my language. I have exhausted the extent of my French vocabulary and I am standing only a few inches from what I want.

The bread's crust is glistening. A thin buttery film. The inside of my mouth is moistening. The smell. The hunger-inducing smell. A shadow casts from my finger and a nervous smile is an internationally accepted indication of my proposed purchase.

The storekeeper carefully lifts the doughy goodness from its keep. I know he is going to say something to me in French. Certainly, it will be the price. I can meet him halfway with the cash in my hands.

My passport. Good.

A receipt from the Chunnel train. Okay.

A few scraps of paper; bubble gum wrappers. It was here!

No wallet. The side pockets of my backpack are emptied, and my wallet is not there! I have been swindled! A victim of a sinister ruse. Robbed. Jacques' kindness hid the nefarious plot of a thief and the presence of his mysterious companion, his smooth-fingered accomplice. My wallet! My driver's license! My bank card! The cash! All gone.

Now the storekeeper is leaning over the counter watching me dissolve into a panicking, loosely clump of coupled cells. I'm about to cry. "No euros," I can barely get those words out of my arid mouth. "I…I don't have money." The storekeeper understands and places the bread back into the display. He must have seen this before. An idiot being somewhere he should not. A simpleton reaping the consequence of his naïveté and voluntary, foolish estrangement from all that is familiar.

A few crumbs fall to the ground as the storekeeper hands me a small pastry. "*Pour vous.*" I am momentarily puzzled. "*Pour vous.*" His hands with fingers firmly pressed together tap his lips in short, fast cycles.

I almost completely miss the meaning of his merciful offer as my fright takes hold of my thoughts. I finally come back to the moment. "*Merci, merci!*" I put the weight back on my shoulders and I am heading to the subway platform. The pounding inside of my chest vibrates the straps on my backpack. I had £50 and another €150, plus my bank card in the wallet. I'm without cash. Without a bank card. I just want to go home.

15

STAY AND SEE

When I got to the hostel, I was somewhat relieved. Before I left England, I had prepaid for the week. Besides that, I had my passport, so I was able to check in and get a room. Nonetheless, I was exhausted, and my thoughts were towards home. Once I had a safe place to leave my backpack, I charged my phone and found a quiet place.

"Hello? What in the hell is the matter with this thing?" I can hear my dad's voice, but he is having difficulty getting the camera to work. "I did! I pushed the damn button! This piece of *mierda* is pissing me off."

"Dad!"

"What? Hold on..." His voice is fading in and out. "Well, get your ass over here and help me if you know so much!"

"Dad!"

I can now hear my mother's voice in the background. "You just slide the little button over that says 'camera,' jackass!"

"You said push! Now, slide? Which is it? This piece of *mierda*!"

"Slide it! It says 'camera' right on it!" I can envision my

mother with her right fist up against her right hip and her head shaking in disbelief.

Finally, I can see a quarter of my father's face.

"Dad! There. You got it." He's gone again. Now he is back again. "Stop! Just stop."

"Tommy! Can you see and hear me?"

"Yes."

"Oh. Okay. Good. How's the trip going, my boy?"

I look around the room. I'm stalling. I always stall. Deep breath. Exhale. "Well, to be honest, it's going terribly, and I want to come home."

"Home? I thought you said…" he is being interrupted. "Will you give me two damn seconds, *coño*! You can talk to him when I'm done. Please! Okay. What's going on, Tommy?"

"I just don't like it here. I wanna come home as soon as I can."

Of course, my father knows me well and surely perceives there is a specific issue bothering me. "Okay. You can come home *pero* why? You just got there."

"I know. I just don't like it."

"Bullshit, *Chico*. What in the hell happened?"

I am stalling again. This time my lips start to quiver. "I… uh…I got pick-pocketed here in Paris. I lost my bank card and all the money I had."

"Holy shit! Do you still have your passport?"

"Yes."

"Did they punch you? Stab you?"

"No, of course not."

"Did you have your PIN written on your card?"

"What? No."

"So, they took your bank card without your PIN and the cash you had with you, *pero* they left you with your health and your passport?"

"Yeah, I guess, but…"

"Then you're okay, son. Learn the lesson and move on."

"This whole trip has been a disaster; I just want to come home." I cannot hide the sobbing. "I can't understand anybody, I got robbed, I can't seem to get from place to place without getting lost. I am miserable."

There is silence on the call. My father is looking behind him to see if my mother is nearby. His stare is one I have seen many times before. He is disappointed in me—at least that is what I am feeling.

"Tommy. What you are feeling is called fear, *papito*. Maybe it's my fault, *pero* you do not like change—it scares the hell out of you. You are always welcome to come home, *pero* I think doing so would be a huge mistake. You will regret it for the rest of your life."

Not even one of my muscles used to make sound twitches in the least. I am paralyzed in fear. My fingers tingle and my arms are numb. My father is right. I would regret not finishing the trip, but I am out of joy.

"Did I ever tell you about your great-great-*abuelo*, Ernesto Luiz Ortega Lopez? The one that came to the U.S. from the island."

"No. I don't think so."

Your great-grandfather lived in Spain when there was a lot of crazy mierda going on. Food was expensive and hard to get because of wars in Europe and he worked with his tío as a horse trainer. He befriended the son of one of the courtiers and enjoyed a few privileges his other friends did not have. He had it made as much as he could. While much of Spain went hungry, he got food from his connected friend. Pero he had also heard about what was going on in the Americas. At that time, Spain still ruled Cuba. So, he got the idea he would get to the United States by first going to Cuba. Chico, there were no cell phones, no telephones, no Internet, or any real way to know what was going on back at home. He was alone and did not have much money, pero he left Spain anyway.

Before he even left Europe, he was arrested for supposedly harming another man's horse. Entonces, you see, he was a horseman and knew all about horses. He knew this other man's horse was sick. When the man saw your bisabuelo touching his horse, he got mad. Of course, the timing of a Lopez is impeccable, and the horse collapsed right there. He spent several days in a dingy prison cell full of rats, roaches, lice, and other nasty mierda until the other man finally dropped the charges. Fortunately, the policeman did not take his money because he had left it at the house where he was staying. He missed his ship, so he had to stay in Portugal for a few weeks until another ship came.

Well, he got on the wrong damn ship and ended up in Africa. No phone. No Internet. Africa. While he was there, he caught malaria and nearly died. Finally, he got on the right ship and started for the Caribbean in the middle of the summer. The ship did not make it. They ran into a big storm several hundred miles from Cuba—probably a hurricane—and the ship started to take on water. Down it went. Luckily, a couple of hours behind, another ship that had missed the storm found the survivors, including your bisabuelo. They all climbed aboard and made it to Cuba the following week. He lost all of his money when the ship sank. The captain of the ship that rescued him was a Spaniard and offered to take your great-grandfather back to Spain if he agreed to work as a deckhand for the voyage. Your great-grandfather was alone and scared. Do you think he wanted to go back home? Hell yes! He absolutely did. Pero he also knew that he needed to see what to him was a new world. He politely declined and found work on a farm in Cuba taking care of the mules.

It would be another four years before he made it to the United States. When he got here, he met your great-great abuela, Marta, and the rest is history, as they say. To hesitate is in your blood. We are risk averse. However, in the end, somehow, the Lopez family has found a way to be successful. You come home now; you won't learn what you need to learn to be as successful as you can be. ¿Comprendes?"

AS MY FATHER finishes this story that I am sure is probably at least fifty percent bullshit, I cannot help but feel he is right. I was going nowhere at home. I feel the future is laced with all sorts of weapons devised to slash me and all I want to do is get on a plane and head home. I want to go home. Still, I need to stick it out a bit longer.

"Yeah. I understand, Dad. I'm here for the week. Once I get a new bank card, I am leaving for the west of France."

"Good choice. Now, talk to your mother before she shits herself."

16

FEAST

Paris is now hundreds of miles of rail behind me. My eyes are much heavier than they have been since I arrived in Europe. At this point, I'd rather sleep than look out of a window. When I do glance out I imagine what it would be like if I just jumped off the train into the terrain. I ask for the strongest coffee on board. It only gives me about thirty minutes of minimal relief. I'm not hungry. My pants are starting to slip down my waist and there are only one or two more belt holes remaining. I post a picture or two on Oratr each day. However, I obscure my zombifying cheeks. I often think to myself "What's the point?" Nonetheless, I keep posting. I have twenty-nine followers now.

Somewhere between Paris and the first stop, I realized that my wallet had much more in it than money and my license. The opening near the crease kept a small charm Katrina gave to me back in high school. I remember putting it there so that I would always feel that she was near. Now, the distance between us expands farther. We are like birds: one flying east and the other west. The image of Jacques standing in front of me like a devil camouflaged in angelic kindness while his ghoul reaches into my backpack sickens me. They took one of the few things keeping my spirit intact in the darkness at night. I swear, if he would just bring that charm back, he could keep the money.

Several more miles down the tracks I started thinking about the gang. Katrina always causes me conflict inside; Kyra perpetually experimenting and testing limits, killing off her former self without a second thought; Pierre desperately searching for respect; Jacob unhinged and willing to put anything in his body; Todd without a care in the world, yet highly intelligent. What was I but someone simply experiencing the interaction of their personalities?

I had to excuse myself from my seat. In the bathroom, I fought the urge to cry. It took me a few minutes, but I finally calmed down. As I sat back down, I curiously felt a little better. There was a bit more diversity in the hue of objects passing outside the window—greener trees, bluer waters, whiter clouds, and lighter shadows. The vibration of the second-class car, as we rolled along the tracks, moved deeper into the bones. The constant clicks and clacks of those around me were clearer. I still had no idea what they were saying, but the sounds were more pronounced. My head was still filled with a soupy fog. At least my senses were at last starting to compensate for it a little.

Not far from the Auray train station was a park. I grabbed a few food items before I stepped off the train and sat down there to see if more of my senses would return to me. In retrospect, I was not looking within, but waiting for something external to myself. I sat for almost an hour and not a soul passed me on the soft, damp field. Finally, I heard the light crushing of grass behind me. I turned but the sun was directly in my eyes. I saluted the fireball to provide some shade for my face. A few moments later, I could make out the one approaching me. A girl. Young. Brown hair and loosely fitting knitted sweater and jeans. Not slender, but not obese. She was perfect as she was. I don't believe in metaphysical stuff, but I swear I could see a white aura shimmering from her body. No words had yet been expressed between us. I could tell she had bubbly spirit if nothing else. There was something in her gait that communicated full gratification. She wore a smile as if worldly weight and stress kept its distance from her. I dared to stare too long and found out quickly that she was not prone to shyness.

"*Voulez-vous ma photo? Je peux poser pour toi si tu veux.*" She tucked her hands on to her hips and twisted her torso.

"Uh. I'm sorry. Something about a photo?"

"*Oui!* I said, do you want a picture? I can pose for you if you wish."

"Picture?"

"*Oui!* A photo picture...what is the matter with you? You have a camera, yes?"

I was completely caught off guard. Nervously, I looked around for a moment like I was searching for a camera. "I'm sorry. I don't understand." My face was passing 400 degrees.

"You apologize a lot *cœur triste,* but you have done nothing wrong. You were looking at me like you wanted a photo. I'll give you a photo." She confidently teases her hair and gets back into her pose.

"I have to find my phone."

She throws her hands in the air signaling defeat. Bending slightly at her hips she touches the tip of my nose with her finger. "You are not much of a photographer, no?"

"I suppose not."

"I also take it you have not been in Auray long? Traveling alone?"

I clench my backpack tightly. "I'm not from here. No. But I came with some friends."

She patrols the entire park turning like a lighthouse beacon. "I see no friends. Maybe they forgot about you, yes?"

I stumble for words as I know she is calling my bluff. Strangely, I think about Kyra, Pierre, and the rest. "Well, no, of course not!"

"Then where are they, *cœur triste*? Perhaps hiding in the trees?"

"No. That's ridiculous."

"Perhaps they are in balloons in the sky?" She knows I'm speaking falsely like an experienced detective.

"Okay! I am traveling alone!"

She grins and sits down next to me taking some of my bread for her own consumption. France is becoming a very queer place to me. Do they always just take what they want? Of course, she has eaten the piece before I can bring myself to words. I witness her throat moving like an ocean wave. Gulp! Down it goes. She was not done! Oh, no. Not this one. Before I could snap at her for my bread she lost all perception of boundaries. Her fingers wrap around my bottle of soda. Having not the least amount of remorse, she delivers a significant sip of the now warming drink into her mouth.

"Ahh! *C'est bon!*"

"Help yourself." Sarcasm pours from my lips.

"I'm Cecile. What's your name?" The previous few minutes are like they did not exist to her.

"Tommy."

"So, Tommy, *cœur triste,* how did you come to picnic in a park in Auray?"

I feel she is asking too many questions. I want to come up with a good backstory that is as believable as it is false; however, for some reason, I am beginning to feel more comfortable with her presence. One thing was for sure: if she was going to steal from me, she wouldn't even try to hide it. That thought was reassuring somehow.

"I am on a year-long trip in Europe. Just traveling, seeing new things."

"Ah! Yes! New things! Very good! Do you know what you are going to experience here in Brittany?"

"I have already been to Britain."

A grimace appears on her face. She shakes her head and takes in all of my ignorance. "No. Not Britain! Brittany. It's a region here in France. The one you are in right now."

My face has to be at least three shades redder. "Oh! I did not know that! No, I am just running away from Paris. I thought I would come to the coast for a while."

"Paris! I love Paris!" I obviously did not share her enthusiasm for the city. "But, I will show you Auray. It's not Paris but it is very nice. Let's get some *crêpes* and cider. I will tell you all about how your Benjamin Franklin came here to our port! Yes?" I am hesitant and first dismiss the offer. Cecile is persistent and finally gets me to agree.

Cecile takes me into the town and near the river that ran through it. I had never seen anybody eat as much as she does. Our table is hidden under plates and bowls containing all sorts of culinary treats. After the third fruit-filled *crêpe* my stomach churned and stretched. She maintains a steady pace of all sorts of *crêpes*: fruit, eggs, sausage, cream, and vegetables. The local region is known for its cider. My head is misjudging the speed and direction of the earth, but Cecile gulps the beverage as if it were mineral water.

Everyone knows her and seems to have great respect for her. She is privileged in the town. No area seems off-limits to her. She stands up in the middle of our meal and goes straight into the kitchen to grab another helping of fruit. The server apologizes to Cecile! I ask Cecile if her family owned the restaurant, and she says no. I'm perplexed but I decide to leave the issue alone. In her company, I enjoy the same popular courtesy. More honestly, I am concerned about the bill that would be soon following.

The conversation itself is enlightening. Cecile tells me that this is the town in France that Benjamin Franklin landed on during his quest to get French support for the war against the British monarchy. I hated history in school. Now hearing it from a foreign perspective was interesting. She makes certain I understand that while we were in France, many of the locals considered themselves just as much Breton as they are French. There is a demonstration of the Breton language, but it sounds like French to me. I asked if it was a dialect of French. Her laughter gives me the answer. I am becoming aware that the cultures and customs of the Europeans are much more diverse than I was led to believe. To my astonishment, Cecile talks about millennia of conflicts between the various identities on the continent. Her take is curious. She does not focus on the destruction nor the misery in history but on the impact on trade and agriculture.

Cecile asks me how long I am going to stay in Auray. I answer honestly—a few weeks. She suggests that I go north from here. I had mentioned that I had some level of faith and so she insists I go to Normandy, another region adjacent to Brittany. On the coast, there is an abbey that has existed for centuries. Early in my journey, I realized the historical impact of religion in Europe. In England, there were large, old churches made of weathered stone in almost every town. France was no different. My hesitation does not affect her enthusiasm. She tells me she would meet me at the train station a few kilometers outside of the abbey. I reluctantly agree.

The bill finally comes to the table, and I start to reach for my wallet. Cecile whispers something into the server's ear and the check never touches the tabletop. I do not say a word. We depart from the restaurant, and she walks me to my hostel.

Tonight I will post some pictures and narration on Oratr. I now have sixty-two followers.

17

THE CLIMB

The sun is still low in the sky barely clearing the rooftops when Cecile and I arrive at this abbey. The approach was frightfully open. A bridge that connects a parking lot to a small island standing in what looks like a plain of mud. It was like a mysterious ocean without water. Spooky. The structure itself is magnificent. To me, it looks like a rock mountain in which a stone structure erupted from a volcano. The top of the building is rectangular with a long point reaching high into the sky. There are jagged edges creating contrast in the ancient architecture and near the bottom several structures that appear as a village sitting on a wall with rounded tops. We have just made it to the wall.

Standing under the entrance—after paying the €10 fee—Cecile encourages me to avoid the fanfare to the right and we go left towards the western side of the island. There are fewer people in that direction. More shadows.

The walk immediately starts to incline. My attention is partially on the vast wasteland surrounding the island. "This is really weird to see a bridge that doesn't go over water to an island not surrounded by water."

The trademark Cecile smile lights up her face. "That would be strange. But there is water here. It's just away for now."

"For now?"

"*Oui!* I would not recommend you go stand out there."

"Why not? I can see a few people out there." My speech is getting more pressured as my breathing rate increases.

"This is one of the fastest tides in France. We are low tide right now. But when it comes back, it returns quickly. The high tide is about 15 meters." I am working on calculations in my head. "About 50 feet." She giggles. I feel stupid again.

"Yeah, I wouldn't want to be caught in that!"

Cecile touches some of the stones as we pass by. "You see this stone?"

"*Oui!*" I am proud of my developing French tongue.

"This is granite from an area about 30 kilome—20 miles away."

"This place is old, right? How did they carry…" I had to take a few breaths, "…how did they get the granite here?"

"The tide!"

"The tide?"

"*Oui.* They would put the granite onto barges and when the tide came in, they would ride the tide here. When the tide went back out, they rode it back."

I am now taking a bunch of pictures. "When was this, like 1800 or something?"

Cecile bursts into laughter. "No, no, *un homme malheureux!* This place goes back to the Eighth Century." I am calculating again in my head. "About 700 A.D.!"

"Oh! Wow!" My face is reddening again.

She gets back on point. "The people who built this did so over many generations. It has been a pilgrimage site for Christians since it was first constructed."

I finally begin to make the connection of this place to our

talk in Auray. "Ah! That is why you wanted me to come here?"

"*Oui!* I found you sad and still. That is why I named you *cœur triste*. It means 'sad heart.' Tommy, you are my sad heart." I could see the compassion in her eyes. "Let's go inside!"

Before us is the entrance to the main building. I have never seen anything like this before. A grand place to house so few of the faithful. The ceilings float high above the ground and the stone floor is cold. Cecile is tugging at my hand. "Let me show you something!" She rushes me through the church and out into an opening. The views are spectacular.

"This part of the church was once enclosed. There was a fire and once it was out, they left it as an open terrace." Even though we had stopped, she continued to shrug at my arm.

"This is beautiful! When was the fire? It must have been long ago because I don't see any charcoal marks."

"Actually, you will never guess when the fire was!"

"The 1800's?" I smirk and lightly giggle.

"Ew! So, close! The fire was in 1776."

I am calculating once more but this time I beat her to the conclusion. "The same year of the American Revolution!" Nailed it!

"*Oui! Oui! Magnifique!* At the same time, an important piece of European history was on fire, you Americans were setting fire to Europe, as well. You see, even as things are destroyed, things are new. There is always something to feast on, it just depends on whether you feast on the dying things or the things being born."

"Did you just give me a sermon?"

Dead silence. Then laughter. "I'm hungry, Tommy. Let's go eat."

18

KINDNESS

We walk back down the circling hill into the village area. I can tell most of the businesses are designed to trap tourists. Cecile admits as much but insists it is that which is above the village that matters. I cannot argue with her.

We enter a restaurant filled with patrons. The best seats provide panoramic views of the bay. Unfortunately, these seats are ordinarily given to those with prior reservations. I asked Cecile if we had reservations. "No." However, just as she answers me, she walks away and speaks with the greeter for a few moments. Less than two minutes later we are sitting in these seats looking out into the expanse of the horizon. We had ordered several dishes of *omelette montoise,* which Cecile assures me is the specialty of the place. She also asks for glasses of muscadet, a wine made somewhere in the region. Not sweet but enjoyable. As we eat, we start to discuss random topics. Eventually, we get to the present moment and commentary of her "Sermon on the Mont."

"So," I uncomfortably begin, "do you prefer eating the dying or the living?"

"Oh, the living without a doubt! Understand what I am

saying. When I say the living, I mean the things in life that are worth consuming." Her smile fades and seriousness takes her face. "Laughter. The future. Happiness. You? You go for the dying things, and it makes your heart sad. Those dying things which are dissolving—you cannot get nourishment from that; you begin to starve."

"But it seems easy for you. Everyone does what you ask them."

"What do you mean?"

"In Auray, you go into the kitchen, no question. Here all of the tables are reserved yet you get one like you own the restaurant."

"Do you want to know what my secret is?"

"Witchcraft?" I nervously giggle. Cecile's eyes roll.

"I feed people, Tommy."

"Feed them?"

"Yes. Feed them. I feed them with the most nourishing food there is: kindness." I am sensing that I am going to feel like an ass again.

"Please. Explain. I think I am a kind person but that doesn't happen to me."

"I walked into that kitchen in Auray because I once helped the owner take time off to bring his mother to the doctor. So, now he says I should help myself when I need to do so. I often watch his mother in exchange for lunch now and then. Kindness. I got a place here because I showed the woman at the front kindness. She just had a rude customer, and everybody has been showing up late for their reservations—yet they are demanding to be seated anyway. I told her I was sorry she was having a bad day and we would come back in an hour. She then told me a couple had canceled a few moments before and she would let us take the reservation instead. Kindness."

"Kindness? That's it?"

"Do you remember when we met, and I ate your bread and drank your soda?"

I look up to act as if I am trying to remember that incident. I always stall. "Um. Yes. I remember something like that."

"It is rude for a person to walk up and do that. But what about a close friend? I could see that you had no trust in other people. Your hand was so tightly gripping your bag that I could see your blood stop flowing. I think when you made up that story about being with friends you actually wanted to believe that. You were starving. So, I broke the barriers down as fast as I could. I ate your food—like an old friend—but I offered a quick snack of kindness in return."

I am now sitting with ten pounds of weight on my lap because it slithered like a snake off my shoulders. Kyra and Katrina had routinely taken my food from me when we were together. I never cared. Cecile was right: I did want them here with me and somewhere in my mind I brought them. It was an easy fib because it rang true in my hopes. Yet, reality was draining me, starving me.

Cecile quickly changes the subject. "*Monsieur,* Tommy. What is next for your journey?"

"I think I will try Germany."

"Ah, Germany. Bavaria is so fun!"

19

ONE LAST VISIT TO PARIS

The trains are punctual in Europe. I suppose this makes sense because most of these towns' crowning objects are enormous centuries-old clocks. Time. Time is a cruel companion. Three circumstances make time especially sadistic. The first is when you have nothing to do. Time will not slow down for you, and your limited amount on earth keeps ticking towards expiration. The second critical situation is when you have too much to do. Time revels in remaining constant. No matter how many tasks need to be completed it will not consider your mental anguish. The final assault is when your heart is broken. All three have this in common: the overwhelming rush of thoughts. Failure of the past and future haunt the captive. There is unyielding heaviness in the chest and tingling in the fingertips. Too much sleep; too little sleep. Too much food; too little food. You end up paralyzed, which only amplifies the time crisis.

~

I LEFT France and crossed the German border. My route took me through Paris, but I did not waste time getting to my next train. I looked for Jacques as I passed through the busier corridors. Cecile's words about kindness float in my head, but I'm not sure I would be able to keep charity at the forefront if I saw his cunning crew. He probably has long spent the money. Upon seeing the charm that Katrina gave me he surely mocked me screeching like a hyena. But I did not see him. However, I did stop by the shop where the keeper was compassionate enough to give me something to eat. He was pleased to see me.

"Bonjour, monisuer! Je m'appelle Tommy. Tu te souviens de moi?" I spoke confidently.

"Ah! *Oui!* Tommy! *Tu peux parler français?"*

I have picked up a few main phrases and words since we last met though I am far from being fluent. I stopped by to thank him again and to pay my debt. *"Très peu! Mais je voulais vous remercier. Et pour vous payer."* I stumbled through those French words.

"Merci! But...please, you do not need to give me any money."

I was shocked like a horse pissing on an electric fence. A huge smile re-shaped my face. "You can speak English?"

"But, of course, sir. I speak very good English!"

I realized he understood every word I said when I was in his shop a month ago. "I was very upset, and you showed me kindness. *Merci beaucoup!"*

I bought a beverage and a loaf of bread. He reached out and hugged me. I picked up my backpack and rushed to the track. The time was 3:41 pm and the train was departing at 3:59–exactly 3:59!

~

I WAS ON A HIGH when I got to the next train that would take me to Munich, Germany. Things were tracking for the better. My backpack was stowed away, and I sat on the comfortable couchette bench seat.

Bzzz. Bzzz.

My Love Katrina has sent you a message.

"Hi. I hope you are having fun in Europe. Where are you now? I wanted to see how you were doing."

"I am in Paris getting ready to head to Munich. How are you?" | Send...

Bzzz. Bzzz.

"Wow! That is great. I wish I could have gone."

"Me too." | Send...

Bzzz. Bzzz.

"I wish I could get away from here altogether."

"Why? What's wrong?" | Send...

Bzzz. Bzzz.

"I'm going nowhere in life. Anthony always works late and is agitated when he comes home."

"That sucks. Can you just avoid him?" | Send...

Bzzz. Bzzz.

"I wish. He comes to find me and it's not pretty."

. . .

My stomach contracts and a rush of heat goes from my belly button to my forehead. He is abusing her. I must correct what I am writing at least six times.

"Can't you just leave?" | Send…

There is a long pause.

Bzzz. Bzzz.

"He probably would never let me. LOL."

All the goodwill I had stored is now exhausted. There is a familiar feeling: Anger. For a moment I think I should cut my trip short and head back home. The urge to slap Anthony across his smug face is growing. I am ready to go to war. Katrina seemed to frequently have me in internal and external combat. I closed my eyes to imagine Katrina's head on my shoulder. Yet, the notion is too painful, and she would only go back to him anyway.

"I'm so sorry, K." | Send…

Bzzz. Bzzz.

"I know."

The subtle rocking of the moving train took nearly an hour to soothe me. I chanted to myself the sentiment Cecile imparted to me: Kindness. The practice was effortless for her. She sent it out and it came back to her in multiplying supply without any attached angst. For me, it was hard labor, and it often returned to me an increasing burden. I have been a constant source of comfort and tenderness for Katrina since high school and to the present. Yet, the rewards have been minimal, and misery has well outweighed them. Is that even love?

20

PEACE

I am face up in my bunk at the hostel in Munich, Germany. I cannot sleep. The snoring around me is not the culprit, nor is it that I am well-rested. On the contrary. I had the most remarkable day and it began upon my arrival.

The hostel here in Munich bristles with people from all over the world. Americans don't really do this sort of travel. The cheapest rooms are dormitories where you sleep among anywhere from two to fourteen other people. These people are from all parts of Europe, Asia, Africa, and Australia, and they are not just those who are young. Whole families are traveling together on what they call a "holiday." I got to my dorm with a slow-moving mind and feet that felt as if they were dragging barbells. I made sure the locks were secured on my zippers and I threaded my leg into and around one of the back straps. In no time, I was drifting out of consciousness.

Several hours had passed and the room had a bluish glow. I lifted my head and I saw the silhouette of a winged creature standing in front of the entryway. I was startled because I had been dreaming that I was in a field running from a forest where awful, demonic sounds echoed, and bolts of lightning were choreographed with explosions from whistling missiles crashing into the ground. Just before I awoke, I had tripped into a missile crater and was tangled in the brush burning within. An arm was reaching into the pit towards my hand. Then, I woke up to see this figure.

"*¡Perdón, señor!*" Her forward momentum ceased suddenly.

I politely reassured the strange woman that I was about to get up anyway. The blue hue dissipated, and I could see that this figure was a woman about my age. Her toes peeked through the straps of her flip-flops. Her jeans fit tightly at her hips and then loosened as they fell to her feet. The blouse she was wearing was splattered with the colors of the rainbow. In her straight, dark hair a blue headband tucked back behind her ears. Her skin was the shade of olives, and it absorbed the light around her. Dangling from her neck was a crucifix having the Christ bleeding upon it. I introduced myself and she told me her name was Angel.

We talked for a few minutes, and she said she was from Colombia and traveling Europe before she started graduate school. Like me she was traveling alone. I immediately felt a strong connection to her, so I invited her to go have dinner with me. She agreed. There was nothing too noteworthy about the dinner, at least concerning the subject matter. We talked about our Latino families and the bizarre habits of our fathers. Most of it was small talk, very comfortable and easy small talk. In the middle of our conversation, I realized that I could not turn away from her deep brown eyes. The entire conversation had steady eye contact and I admit I began to feel a closeness forming between us. I dared not say anything to her, but I knew that I was interested in spending as much time with her as I did with Cecile, albeit in a very different way. Angel had a sense of humor but was not nearly as forward as Cecile. She was measured. Quietly confident. Explicitly smart. Her ability to talk about big ideas wooed my interest. Angel asked me open questions and said very little in response. She was absorbing what I was saying, not just the words, but the intent of the words. Even though the vast majority were small talk, the impact was massive. I had not felt this sort of connection since high school. My chest lifted outward and a gooey stew formed on my palms.

The evening wore on and we continued to have a pleasant series of conversations. Favorite movies. Weird experiences. Family quirks. Steins of beer emptied and were filled again. Eventually, it was time to return to the hostel. I purposely walked slowly to extend the evening as long as possible. I was looking for any opportunity to come up with a reason to hang out a little longer. Angel finally invited me to visit the concentration camp museum just outside of town. I quickly agreed though I had little interest in history.

We snuck quietly into the dormitory and tipped-toed between the sounds of light snoring. I crawled into my bunk and she into hers.

I was now at one-hundred-sixty followers.

21

THE CAMP

Angel and I had an early breakfast in the basement of the hostel. In a rush of impromptu curiosity, I watched her interact with her food. The plate was filled and organized with purposeful care. She had fruit, some bread, butter, and apricot jam. None of the ingredients touched each other and were ordered in degrees of sweetness. First the bread, then the butter. Next the fruit and then the jam. She first took the butter and spread it thinly on the bread. After that, she cleaned the knife on the edge of the bread and layered generous amounts of jam on top of the butter.

She placed the bread back down onto the plate and carefully selected bites from the fruit. There was clarity in her actions. No indecision to be found. The bread never interfered with the consumption of the fruit. Angel left the bread to absorb the butter and jam as she finished the fruit. The bread was given the same consideration. Nothing was mixed in between the bread and her mouth except a few words of conversation. I watched in astonishment. I had switched off between my bread and juice, my juice and fruit. I realized how chaotic I was even in something as routine as eating. I first wondered if she needed to have such symmetry in her life that she would have such a specific obsession. The more I observed the more I came to settle on the fact she was simply content and desired to enjoy the flavors and nourishment of one food at a time. We finished the meal with a strong cup of coffee and headed out into the brisk morning wind.

On the way to the museum, I noticed Angel was tightly pressed against my side and clenching my arm. I could smell the bouquet of sweet flowers and spices steaming off her skin. A flightiness settled into my stomach, and I began to converse with myself in my head. I realized she was simply cold and using my body for heat to warm herself. I was warming up, too—on the inside.

I asked her what our destination was, and she reminded me it was the Dachau Concentration Camp—a place of suffering and a reminder of what humanity could do to one another with minimal convincing. I remembered hearing about something like this in a class once or twice. I was woefully ignorant. In my head, I thought it was some manicured building with exhibits neatly placed in rows. We departed the bus and started walking towards the gates. She squeezed my hand tightly and confided she was uncomfortable being near a place with a history of such death and agony. Angel insisted it had a visceral effect on her and that she could literally feel God's Grace being pulled through her pores and into the unseeable suffering that lingered in the air. One of her hands clasped over mine and the other rubbed the crucifix around her neck.

Once we entered through the gates, I realized my understanding of Dachau was grossly inadequate. There was a building, but there was also wire fencing, rectangular guard towers rising over oval-shaped light posts, and a large open field. I could see moisture build-up and glaze over Angel's eyes. I put my arm around her. My shoulder countered the gravity tugging at her head. We walked into the field towards the steps of the main structure.

The entire grounds were haunting. The structures stood as grotesque souvenirs of the terror of global conflict—the cheapening of humanity into a machine of war and death. I found the word "camp" to lack accuracy. The crematoria and the ditches running from tower-to-tower did not seem to me to be landmarks in a former "concentration camp," but of a cruelty factory. All the time, Angel sought my shoulder as a refuge during the most dreadful realizations of what happened there. About halfway through our day, I realized I had experienced this role as a convenient comforter before. Katrina used to do the same thing when the world made her sad. The circumstances with Angel were somehow different. Astronomically different. She was not mourning the loss of a misguided, corrupted love but the corruption of a world that could choose to show love yet did not. She was not caught in the self-pity religion of God-why-me-ism but in the purest of conscientious skepticism of God-why? The selfishness I battled internally was not there with Angel. There was a wholesomeness about my motives. Many nights I wished for Katrina to be in pain so that her touch could soothe mine; however, there with Angel, I felt no guilt and no regret. I wanted her pain to end forever, not to linger. The act seemed more genuine; more effective. I was feeding Angel the flesh of the living, not dying things.

I WAS SO COMPLETELY ignorant about the world. Not only what I could see, but what I could not see. Things that are not known through some observation or experience, yet can be revealed in a new experience. I vaguely remembered being in a class listening to my 9th grade teacher talk about the holocaust. The events seemed so unbelievable and tucked far under history. Thinking deeply about it never really happened for me. Honestly, I thought this was something that happened hundreds of years ago. Indirect education could not reach me. The pictures showed the horrible results of what some people called the Nazis did to other people somewhere far away. I could see suffering. I could see death. I could see evil. Yet, it was not my problem. People today wouldn't do that. We were more aware.

My lack of empathy hid a million truths. There were laws of nature gluing these acts of unkindness together. I had heard about the "moral compass," and what is considered doing the right thing. It seemed to me that a compass always pointed in the same direction. If you turn, the needle keeps pointing to the same spot. Magnetic north. What happens if there is no magnetic north, morally speaking? What if there are things around that interfere with the internal compass? One of these two situations must have been how an entire modern civilization did what it did. Believing this provides some comfort. However, the reality is that many had a clear shot to moral north. Despite this, the same many participated in killing and destruction. A straight line to the moral north is a constructed hypothesis. The truth is the law of nature does not have rails or bumpers to keep us narrowly on target. King David has been recorded in history as a good man. Someone seeking God's own heart. David was also a murderer and morally repugnant in many of his actions. What other evils did he do that we don't know about? Within his own heart, there was a war. A war that is common to all, but we are placed in different parts of the battlefield. Some of us on the front lines; some of us in tents far from the firefight. I never realized that until I came to this damned place.

~

The Dachau Cruelty Factory opened my eyes to many larger notions. Cecile taught me the profitability of kindness. Now, her definition seemed incomplete and only a partial understanding. Yet, what was I missing? Why did people here willfully practice such disregard for kindness? I drifted distant from the moment, and I did not notice that Angel had walked away from me. When I realized she was not by my side, I searched the area and found her in meditative paralysis. Her body barely moved. If she were not standing, I would have thought she was asleep. Her breath was shallow, and her hands hovered near her hips with the palms open and relaxed. I did not want to bother her, so I sat watching for a few moments. She finally lifted her head and cheerfulness returned to her. I was perplexed. For the past three or four hours she marched the campus with a burdened soul. As if a switch had been reversed, Dachau had lost its ability to affect Angel. She took her coat from my hands and pressed her jovial body against mine, kissed me on the cheek, and reclaimed my arm.

The gates of Dachau vanished behind us, and we made our way back to Munich. On the train, we both caught up on our digital lives. I posted a few pictures on Oratr and she sent a few messages to her mother.

We are back at the hostel, and we are both exhausted. I collapse on my bunk and she on hers. I asked her what we were going to do the next day. She lifts her head and glances across the four or five bunks between us with her stoic eyes. "Anything with you."

I smile. I attempt to reply to her, but I drift away before I can say another word.

There are 980 followers.

22

A PIECE OF THE HEART

The past two months in Bavaria left my mind in the greatest chaos it had ever been. Not in the way I had long experienced where I resisted every new moment and in frantic futility tried to bring the past to the present. I started to find myself starving in the present, but also learning how to eat. There are still thoughts within me that want to reassert dominance and drag me back down; however, I am acquiring skills to bring a bit more peace through internal dialogue. Angel taught me that. I told her about most of the struggles I have had in my life. That is when I discovered she was training to be a clinical psychologist. By far, I talk the most in our discussions. She patiently listened to my woes and nodded. I felt that I could tell Angel anything without judgment—or the ultimate result of me being required to absorb her woes, as well. I loved to listen to Angel talk about her passions., one of her passions was to simply listen.

My heart was getting sad again. Time in Bavaria was ending. She needed to return to Colombia to get ready to start graduate school. I decided that I should move on, too.

We sat on the floor of the Munich station waiting for the

next scheduled train to the airport. Our last few moments are quickly ticking away, and I foolishly brought up Katrina again.

"I'm sorry, Angel. We should talk about something else." I was not happy with myself. There are many other things I wanted to say to her, but I had already blurted out that name.

Angel turned her head towards the crowd pressing her lips tightly together and shook her head for a few seconds. *"Never give all the heart, for love."* A thin smile returned to her face and her eyes locked onto mine.

"Never what?"

"'*Never give all the heart, for love.*' W.B. Yeats. The wise words of a poet. Do you know what happens to the one that gives all of his heart for love, Tomás?" Her palm lightly touched my chest where the heart is.

"No."

Her other hand reached for my face. "He loses. He well knows the cost, but still gives his whole heart to the object of his desire—and he loses. It causes him to lose everything and leaves him wounded and bleeding. It takes away his peace."

I felt a tear rolling down my cheek. "It hurts to lose."

"And the skin around the wound heals to a scar. You have to learn how to accept your scars and dare to risk further injury, but never give the full heart. Keep some of your heart for yourself."

I heard Cecile's voice synchronize with what Angel had told me. Together they gave me the missing piece. I had long seen kindness as an expression and an action. However, kindness is more than that. It is a state of self-existence. I rarely had kindness for myself. All of my love was dedicated to the external and left none for myself. "How do I accept those scars?"

Both of her hands gently caressed my cheeks. Her eyes were inches from mine. Our breathing coordinated. She exhaled, and I inhaled. My brain became woozy; my body numb. I'm intoxicated. "Don't fear the future. Embrace the present. Keep your heart and mind in the moment." In the background, I heard with clarity German announcing her train had arrived and is ready for boarding.

I closed the remaining distance and our lips softly met.

"I think I am giving my heart again."

"Uh, huh. *Sì, un poco.*"

"I do know this: when you get on that train, you are going to take my heart with you to Colombia." I paused. "Forgive me if I keep a little part of it for myself."

Angel lurched forward and squeezed my body one last time. "I don't mind at all, *mi amor*."

She boarded. The train started to move and we waved to one another one last time. My sight of her fades as she dipped behind the curvature of the earth. She left with a large piece of my heart. The speck of her heart with me left an abundance of peace.

23

WORD FROM HOME

"*Mi amor,* what are you up to now?" I haven't heard my dad's voice for almost a month and a half.

"I'm in Vienna getting ready to head to Poland."

"Wow. Okay. Fill me in on wha—what? Yes, it's Tommy!" I can hear my mother's voice in the background. "I have no idea where it is...I don't know check inside your *culo*! Sorry. What have you been up to since we last talked?" Mom chimes in again. Her voice louder and her tone more demanding. "*¡Coño!* Give me two seconds, *mami*! *¡No me jodas*!"

"Shut up!" My mother sharply retorts.

"Is this a bad time?" I laugh.

"Your mother. Every time I am talking on the phone, she has to find something or needs something and she thinks I keep track of all of this *mierda*. You could call me at 3 AM and she will wake up and ask me where the car keys are. *¿Necesito las llaves? ¿Necesito las llaves? ¡Cállate, perra!*" The last part he says softer because he knows better. I'm giggling outside, but inside I am roaring. Nothing has changed at home. Nothing at all. "Go ahead, *Principe,* sorry."

"After I left Munich, I went to Switzerland. Then I went to Italy for a little bit. I basically just took the train around there for a couple of weeks. Saw Rome, the leaning Tower of Pisa, and ate pizza in Naples. That was fun. Then, I came up here to Austria. Learned a bit more German."

"German!" My dad in his not-so-sensitive way always said German was the Arabic of Europe with a lot of "ahkkkkks" and "klaaaaas."

"Ja, Deutsch. Ich finde, es ist eine schöne Sprache."

"Oh, yeah? *Ich bahkkkkkkks und klaaaaaas Schmidt bahkkkindorph."*

I burst into laughter again. "Wow! Impressive! I'm not familiar with that particular dialect, but I think you just said something about having small private parts."

"Where's the lie? Huh?"

"Good point."

"Have you heard from that *chica* you met in Germany?" I can hear a genuine hope in his voice.

"A few times. She puts comments on my Oratr posts, and we text every so often. But she's in Colombia."

"I see. You really like this girl, huh?"

This is where I usually stall. But I don't this time. "I do. I really do. But like I said: Colombia."

"I hope you can see by now that as big as the world seems to be, it is a small place, *mijito*. You are learning, *pero* you have a lot more to learn."

I know exactly what he is trying to say, but I am not ready to take the lesson in just yet. If I have learned anything on this journey, it is that my father has an uncanny ability to predict what lies ahead for me next. To be honest, I think I am now terrified of him. He is like a fortune teller with hairy legs, gassy guts, and beer breath.

"I'll get there, dad." I think for the first time I truly believe I will.

"You will, you will."

I say goodbye, and I hang up the phone.

Bzzz. Bzzz.

"Hey, Tommy."

"Hello." | Send

Bzzz. Bzzz.

"How's your day?"

"Fine. In Austria." | Send

Bzzz. Bzzz.

"Nice."

"Yeah. It's beautiful." | Send

Bzzz. Bzzz.

"I wish I was in Austria."

"Yeah." | Send

Bzzz. Bzzz.

"I don't know why I decided to get married and stay here."

I SURVEY MY BODY. Nothing much beyond the functions required to sustain life. No sweat. No tearing into my stomach. No restlessness. Peace. The phone vibrates with a few "?" as to inquire if my attention is on her. I tell myself that I will not answer. There is no need to repeat the decision. I put the phone into my pocket as I board the train to *Kraków,* Poland. The trains are so punctual here.

I have just over 2,000 followers!

24

LIFE

K*raków* has many wonders. Like many ancient European cities, the architectural history spans centuries with each age leaving its mark on the world. I am pleased to find out that the city avoided much of the destruction other cities suffered during past wars. I wonder if that is because there are so many churches in the city? There seems to be a church on every street corner.

My first impression of the Polish people was that they lacked the same welcoming culture as others in Europe. But the more I am here, the more I am changing my mind. I was fortunate enough to find a middle-aged woman with good English. She told me that what appears to be a standoffish nature is partly a cultural leftover from the days of Communism. She explained that Polish people love to talk and celebrate, but in those days you did not talk to anyone you did not know in public for fear the Russians were listening. After our conversation, I decided to not force any conversations and to respect their culture. Within days, I met a few Polish acquaintances who invited me into their apartments–what they call a flat around here.

The whole ordeal made me think about what I wanted to do when I got back to the States. A few months ago, I would have been satisfied returning to work lifting tile onto the bed of some pickup truck. Now, I am not too sure. For a long time, I wondered how Kyra could reinvent herself so many times. In high school, she was a chameleon. Every year she was into something else. At the time, I admired her for being in touch with her own desires but there was still an anger that burned inside of her. So much was the heat from her displeasure I was scared of her. I once even had a nightmare that she was chasing me in a cornfield with a black sickle. It seems to me now that while she always understood she was complex, she never really could make out what truly made her happy. She ferociously consumed dying things. The only way she could cope with the starvation was to reinvent herself and distance herself from the shell she left behind. She knew she was searching, but never really knew for what she was searching. Here I am, not too long before I return home, just now realizing that I am searching, too. But for what?

In a bit of self-reflection, I wandered away from the hostel and into the city center, the *Rynek Główny*. The Cloth Hall has several restaurants so I go there for my new favorite soup, *żurek*, and a beer.

"Nein! Es Ist zwischen deinen Beine, Arschloch!" A roar of laughter a few tables from me and captures my attention. Three young men are jostling and pressing their palms against each other. I am not fully fluent in German but the one said something about the other's legs and called him an asshole. The one that is the apparent asshole leaps up from his chair frantically slapping his private parts. The other two fall to the ground in hysterics. One of them that fell to the ground, a jolly chap, catches me looking their way.

"American! American! The jolly chap is pointing at me. I point to my chest. "Yes! American, right?"

"Uh. *Ja, ich bin ein Amerikaner.*"

"Oh! *Du kannst Deutsch sprechen?*" He claps his hands and turns to his comrades in amazement. I immediately go back into my language shelter.

"No. No. *Nein*! I know very little. Do you know English?"

"*¡Sí, hablo ingles!*" The three are erupting in laughter again. I guess this is a joke. I smile. The jolly one walks towards my table. "I am joking, yes? I speak English."

"How did you know I am an American?"

"American football!" He growls out the last part of the word football. "Do you play?"

I am still quite confused. "Well, I, uh…"

His hand raises from his hips and the index finger extends towards my backpack. Of course, the patch!

"Ah! The football helmet patch!"

"Yes! Yes! American football!" He growls at the ending again.

"No. I am just a fan." His other fingers join his index finger and he reaches closer to me.

'"Bernard Hoffer. I am from Hamburg." I'm getting the opinion that Bernard is both friendly and into American football. I politely introduce myself, as well. He waves for his other friends to join. "This is Hansel Krueg from Berlin, and this is Dietrich Gertz from Shitsburg" They all start laughing again.

The one called Dietrich takes his left hand and clamps down on Bernard's right nipple and twists. Bernard is screaming and laughing at the same time. Hans takes Bernard's other nipple and twists. Dietrich can hardly keep his breath; he is giggling so violently. Then, Hans reaches over and takes hold of Dietrich's right nipple. Bernard immediately follows with a counterattack seizing one of Han's and Dietrich's nipples. Dietrich counters by grabbing Han's other nipple. In front of me are three German grown men latched tightly onto each other's nipples.

Dietrich screeches out, "Do you know what this is called?" His face is turning the color of blood.

"Drei Idioten?" I figure they would not be insulted. They all cackle at a higher pitch.

"No. This is called a Swedish Standoff! Who will piss their pants first? Ow! Ow!"

Hans counts off, *"Drei, Zwei, Eins!"* In unison, they all rip their fingers away falling to the ground in agonized giggles. Consoling their breasts, the three sit down and order more beer.

Bernard's arms are on a multi-directional swivel as he speaks. "You look like a 'Karl' to me. Yes! *Karl Ziel Verloren*!" The other two snicker like hyenas and join in, *"Karl Ziel Verloren!"*

I know enough German to make out what they are saying. "Karl, but lost?"

"Karl is a very distinguished name." Hans flexes his chin towards his mouth and looks at Dietrich before rolling his eyes.

I'm a bit bothered that these blokes see me as lost. Lost from what? A breeze swooshes through the forest of umbrellas giving me an opportunity for a counterstrike. Hans' hat begins to dislodge from his skull, and he responds in haste. Just as his hand gets to his head, an elbow collides with his beer. It tumbles to the ground.

"Hans von Verlor Bier!" The verbal timing is impeccable. A microsecond of silence passes and then we erupt into a ferocious guffaw. Dietrich collapses to the surface again and Bernard slaps Hans on the back of his head. Tears are raining down my cheeks and I have an erratic breathing rhythm. My childish anger manifested in a spontaneous joke about a lost beer.

Everyone is in such a roar, and I feel as if I am having an out-of-body experience. The rumble seems like it is subsiding but then Dietrich, contorted on the ground, forces so much gas from his intestines that the low frequency echoes off the stone walls. An ancient mystery, but it seems all men from around the world cannot resist finding the humor in a loud public fart. We are now four dudes on the floor clinching our bellies and desperately sucking oxygen from the air.

Bernard finally makes out a few pressured syllables, "*Dietrich von Verlorenes Arschloch!*"

"I think I pissed my pants," I'm in splendid suffocation.

"Karl, *Karl von Verlorener Pisse!*" People are starting to stare at us now from across the square. I have only made the acquaintance of these guys for about ten minutes, and it seems like we are senior-year fraternity brothers.

A shadow cuts the intensity of the lights and a figure emerges holding four new beers. We erupt in simultaneous but uncoordinated applause.

"A toast to our new American friend and to life!" Bernard's arm is stretched up to the rafters.

"Here, here!" Hans and Dietrich also lift their glasses. I follow.

"To *den Amerikaner und drei Arschlöcher!*" Nothing seems to offend these dudes. In fact, they seem to take the playful insult as a welcomed moniker.

Dietrich gulps his beer and wipes his mouth with his sleeve. "Karl, what are you doing here in *Kraków*?" I have learned that this is a genuine question among travelers.

"I've been traveling for almost a year. Almost done. I am leaving back to the States in about a month." I show them my Oratr page. Hans forces Dietrich and Bernard into a tight huddle and motions me to take their picture. I do.

"Now, we are celebrities, too!" Hans jokes, Dietrich snaps

his fists sharply into Han's midsection. "Oomph!" Laughter ensues as Hans doubles over gasping for air.

Bernard removes his nerdy eyeglasses and cleans the lenses with a dry napkin. "Where have you been so far?" I answer his question matter-of-factly. He lightly hammers his chin with the knuckles of his clenched right fist. "Hmmm. Those are good places. You are still searching, yes?"

Searching? I am not totally sure what he means by this. I know what I was thinking when I left the hostel, but they wouldn't know anything about that. My mouth touches the edge of the glass and I take a sip of beer. "Why do you say I am searching?" I place my beer back down.

Bernard opens his palms facing the sky and his shoulders lift towards his ears. "You have been traveling in Europe for a long time and yet, here you sit by yourself with a look of contemplation on your face. You are thinking about something. You're searching."

Desperately, I am trying to understand what he means. I'm not sure if it is a translation thing or if he is just being purposefully mysterious. I point towards Hans, "Is he searching?"

"Nein."

My elbow comes to rest on the table, and I point to Dietrich, "Is he searching?"

"Nein."

All at the table are silent now. The other three are giving me a direct stare. This situation has transformed into an interrogation. "I'm sitting here with you. What do you mean: I'm searching?"

Hans taps the table with his fingertips. "What did you expect to find when you came to this place tonight?"

"I don't know. Nothing really. Just a place to relax, I guess."

Dietrich enters the fray. "When you got here, did you find nothing?"

"No. I mean I did not have an agenda when I decided to come here."

Bernard has been sipping his beer but then reasserts himself. "No agenda? Of course, you had an agenda. Everybody has an agenda. Even if your agenda is not to have an agenda. That's the agenda."

"I see what you mean, but I am not sure where you are going with this."

Hans takes the floor again. "We don't believe in coincidences. All three of us believe in purpose. There is a purpose for air. There is a purpose for beer. There is a purpose for the birds and the flies. Most of all, there is a purpose for life."

I think Hans has just said something profound. I'm not sure what, but the words seem as if they had, well, purpose. Both of my elbows are on the table and my fingers intertwine. My eyes turn to Dietrich.

"The fear of death and failure is easy to read on your face." I knew Dietrich was next. I found the pattern. "But, you also look like a person who has found a new hope and is looking for where he should go next." I think about Angel immediately.

Bernard's turn. "Whatever it is you just thought about. That is part of the answer to what you are searching for. It is not worth just living life. You have to find purpose for it, too."

I make a joke to slice the tension. "You are not going to offer me something in return for my soul are you?" They laugh.

"Would you sell your soul, Karl?" Hans leans in towards me.

"I don't think so."

Dietrich smiles. "Good. Then why would you give it away for free?" Boom! A bomb goes off in my body pressing my organs against my bones and skin. They nailed it! It's my soul. That is what I've been searching for these last months.

Bernard brings the idea to bed. "Your soul, Karl. Fight for all of it. That is what represents you where your body cannot go. It's a natural law, my friend. It's what people perceive about you but cannot see. If you don't keep your soul, then you are a ghost. Is your purpose to haunt or to live?"

"Who in the hell are you guys?"

"Friends," Bernard confesses. "We saw you before you saw us. We were talking about you before the bug landed on Dietrich's crotch. We had decided you were a man in search of something big."

Hans demands we stop. "Shh! Shh!" He stomps his feet twice and then on the third contact a rumbling noise vibrates from between him and his seat. The rancid smell spreads faster than contagion. Dietrich, Bernard, and I spring out of our chairs to scatter. We return to laughter and juvenile behavior.

Five-thousand-eight-five follow me now.

25

PURIFICATION

The Baltic Sea is like a body of water I have never seen before. It's cold. It's spooky. It's the darkest blue. The white sand disappears into the depths, and I imagine it as an ancient graveyard for Vikings, pirates, and sea bandits. I'm watching the waves crash onto the shore and my mind is still, calm. Over to my right, about 20 feet away, a man is walking with a young child. The man is pointing out birds flying over the shoreline. He keeps repeating the same word over and over again. For some reason, I think about Papa D and the things he pointed out to me. My fear of change. The wasting of my life. That day in his office, he was showing me the metaphorical birds that were flying over. I was too immature to understand. I didn't have a word yet to label the soaring fowl. He said he liked me too much, so he had to fire me. I now understand why. Those winged creatures were Cardinals, Blue Jays, Robins, and all the birds that symbolize good fortune.

Dad has told me that Papa D's health is getting worse. He has been in and out of the hospital a few times since I left–complications with diabetes. When I get back, my first stop will be to see Papa D. The rotund grumpy man with a heart of diamonds. He is not technologically savvy–or should I say, he has an aversion to it–so, I have only talked with him twice since I have been here and that was during the early part of the trip. To him, I owe a hefty debt for the good fortune that has found me.

~

THE BREEZE IS A BIT COOL, so I walk further up the beach until I approach a wall that follows the edge of a grassy lot.

"*Dzień dobry!*" I hear a young man's voice as I almost step on him. He is a thin fellow, no more than 130 pounds. He sits with his legs folded and almost perfect posture. The tight elastic shirt with evaporating sweat clues me in that he has been exercising.

"Zen doebray." My Polish pronunciation needs help. "Good afternoon."

"Good afternoon, Canadian?" I gently correct him. "Oh! What brings you to *Gdańsk*?" I tell him the story so far. About Papa D. The misfortunes in Britain and Paris. About Cecile, Angel, Hans, Dietrich, and Bernard. He nods his head and never breaks eye contact with me. I have just met this chap, yet he seems familiar.

"Are you from *Gdańsk*?" I probe him for information.

"No, not originally. I was born in a town called *Lubawa*." Of course, I have no idea where that is but I continue to listen to his story. "I left there when I was about 10 years old. My parents died in a car crash, so I moved to *Gdańsk* with mom's brother."

"Uh, you mean your uncle? Can I sit down?"

"Of course!" He shifts slightly to make room for me. I lower myself to the ground. The briskness is immediately removed. I am shielded from the wind and the waning sun is peeking through the clouds. As I come to rest, he introduces himself.

"My name is Alexandr, but people call me Alex." I still cannot make sense of it, but I keep thinking I know this person. There is intrigue.

Soon the stars will be coming out and the temperature will dip. I offer to go have some drinks with Alex. He declines. He does not drink alcohol. I then see if he would like to grab a pizza. He declines. He does not eat what he calls unclean food. In a final attempt, I ask if he would like to go get a coffee. He declines again. He does not like to ingest caffeine or added sugar and the bitterness of black coffee is too much. Alex reaches into his bag and retrieves some nuts and chopped vegetables. Raw broccoli, carrots, and cauliflower.

"You are really into eating healthy." My words come out partly as a common observation and partly in judgement.

"The world is full of sickness and I try not to invite that into my body voluntarily."

Ordinarily, I would be done with such a person. "Do you eat ice cream?"

"No."

"Why not?"

"I minimize milk, but it's mostly the sugar."

"Sugar-free ice cream?"

"No."

"Why not?"

"I don't eat artificial sweeteners."

"Hot dogs?"

"No. I don't eat processed foods."

"Potato chips?"

"No. Same reason."

"Chocolate?"

"No. Cocoa beans contain caffeine."

I'm marginally frustrated. What can you do with such a

person? Yet, I remain drawn to him. I don't know why. I decided to challenge him further and ask why he is so restrictive with his diet.

"This is my temple. It is mine to destroy or to build. I made the choice to build it several years ago." His eyes are truthful and is quite comfortable with this choice.

"Ok. But why not treat yourself every once in a while? What would a candy bar every now and again hurt?"

"Do you have anything in your life that you struggle to distance yourself from?" My frustration becomes discomfort. "The one or two things that if you let yourself partake just once you know you won't stop?"

"I suppose."

"For me, that is self-destruction. Bad food. Bad drinks. Chemicals. When my parents died, I was lost. For a couple of years, I seemed okay, but I started to eat to ease the pain."

I realize the cause of the interpersonal connection. Alex reminds me of Jacob. A tear forms in my eye and my mouth quivers.

"Does that make you sad, Tommy?" I get my composure back and I reveal my feelings concerning Jacob. Alex confides in me his whole story.

I ate and ate. By the time I was 14, I weighed 72 kilograms. By the time I was 17, I was over 90 kilograms. When I looked in the mirror, the pain grew. I started to drink beer and liquor. At 18, I was out of control. Jacek–the man who took me in–did his best. He was welcoming and encouraging. He was a mariner and spent a great deal of time at sea. I tried to make friends, and I did, but they were unkind and as I added weight, they became mean. Some would even tease me about my parents being dead. Others joked that I must have eaten them. It hurt. I spiraled downward. I just wanted to ease the pain. I did not want to destroy myself, yet in temporarily easing the pain, I nearly did. Almost every night I was drunk by the time I went to bed. I woke up feeling alone and physically ill. I got to the point where I was sure I was going to die. That drove me to eat and drink even more. Then something happened.

One morning, Jacek was walking out the door getting ready to go to sea. He stops and looks at me and says, "I'm sorry." I didn't know how to react to that. Why was he sorry? He dropped his bags and hugged me. I was unclean. Hadn't showered in several days. I hadn't brushed my teeth in probably weeks. My clothes were soiled and unwashed. I smelled like a dead animal. Despite all of this, he hugged me. For the first time since my parents died, I felt someone cared. Well, I went to my room and cried for probably three or four hours. Something came out of me. A darkness. A disease. My mind cleared. I had been purified of the negative thoughts. I knew that I needed to do the same for my temple. The pieces of me that I rejected returned to me. I had to make the choice to end the pain and not just hide it.

I imagine your friend had similar feelings. I turned to food; he turned to drugs. But the food would have killed me eventually, too. No, you didn't spend day after day with Jacob, but you talked to him from time to time. You were a mariner trapped in your own sea. That is not your fault. In the end, your friend made his choice. Believe me, he got to the point where he cried for hours and hours. He did not release the darkness. Perhaps it was the addiction to those chemicals that made it harder for him. That was not your choice or responsibility to save him. You can only say you care. Show that you care. You did that. I will not allow those demons back into me.

I enjoy being 67 kilograms; having the energy to work on what stresses me; and waking up feeling positive and alert. Your friend is refined in his passing. It's time that you are refined here on earth.

. . .

AN UNCONTROLLABLE WAVE oscillates between my toes and head. I break down sobbing uncontrollably. A grown man, bawling his eyes out in public. I cover my face and try to stop the heaving. Alex encourages me to keep going. I do. Wave after wave cycles through my body.

I'm finally starting to feel better and the purge ends. My sleeves are soaked from wiping my eyes.

"Did you feel it? The last gram of guilt leaving your body?" Alex places his hands on my shoulder like an older brother.

The guilt is gone. I did not even realize I had guilt about Jacobs' death. Now there is no question. But it is gone. The sensation is hard to describe. This was not weight falling from my shoulders or butterflies in my stomach. There was a sense of purification that Alex talked about. I think I have my soul back in its whole.

Alex smiles. "*Nowa dusza*! You are now a new soul. Make the best of it."

The night has come and Alex needs to go home. We hug and part ways. A few feet away I stop. I retrieve my phone and open Oratr. I type out six words, add a selfie, and send it to my 11,972 followers.

"Meet me in Prague next Friday"

26

PRAGUE

I arrived in Prague several hours ago. Entering the ancient city, I was busy updating my Oratr account. I did not see much. When I finally looked around as we approached the train station, I was not initially impressed. The station looked like an abandoned factory with two metal half-dome structures covering the tracks. I disembarked the train and headed to the main station. This area seemed much more contemporary with digital marquees and a well-lit hall covered by brick-red ceiling tiles. Familiar fast-food restaurants polluted the station. I had no desire to eat there.

While the main rail was adequately modern, the local trams looked to me like something out of some of those movies my father watched. The noses were rounded as were the headlights. Nonetheless, the system was sufficient to get me where I wanted to go. I had found a hostel not far from the St. Charles bridge. There I found the old-world charm I had expected. The bridge boasts numerous musicians playing different styles of music. You can hear the guitars, percussion, singing, and wind instruments on every inch of the bridge. As one fades in the distance, another melody greets you.

Medieval architecture and ornaments surround the entire place adding effect to the sounds of music. On that bridge, my entire perception of Prague changed, and I absorbed the energy into my soul.

The night has come, and I am standing at the threshold of the club. I maintain the hope that the place will be full of my Oratr followers, yet I also accept that few, if any, will come. A flight of stairs leads to the second level, so I start my journey up. People are passing me as I climb; however, nobody says a word. As I am turning the final corner, I can hear voices chattering. This is it! I go straight to the bar. No one pays me any mind. I order a drink and fight the urge to feel devastated.

The bartender places my order on a clean napkin and can tell my mood is not what it should be in such a place.

"Friend, this is a place to be happy!"

I immediately smirk because I know what I must look like. "Of course! I am very happy. I was just hoping that a group of some of my acquaintances would be here." I stir the Vodka into the orange juice.

"More people will show up. You will feel more happy, yes?"

My head nods. "I will be happy either way." He turns to take another order.

The first sip of the drink is stiff and my teeth clinch. I'm looking around the club in hopes that someone will notice me. So far, nothing. Another larger sip. The bartender gives me his attention again.

"How many people are you expecting?"

"I really don't know. Maybe two; maybe 10? This was kind of short notice."

"Well, I hope they show. Perhaps you will be lucky like the guy everyone is waiting for upstairs. That is going to be a party." He wipes the bar top with a white, wet rag and shrugs his shoulders.

"Excuse me." I set my drink down and some of the vodka-orange juice sloshes onto the bar top. "Did you say they are waiting for someone upstairs?"

"Yes. He is supposed to be some popular guy on the internet. At least twenty people are up there."

I SPRANG up and hastily placed a thousand Koruna on the bar. The crowd has been a bit thicker since I arrived so I am navigating the human mass. I start my way up the stairs and I'm high as the stars. Breaching the threshold of the next level I hear a cackle of familiar voices yell, "Karl!" Dietrich walks up to grab my nipple. I swat his hand away and close in for the bear hug.

"What took you so long, *Arschloft*?" Bernard is in his interrogation stance.

"I was lost; now I am found!" The three of us bust out into hysterics.

Another soothing sound ripples behind me. "*Bonjour*, Tommy, I've missed you *mon cœur*." I spin around. It's Cecile! My arms surround her body and I give hundreds of mini kisses to her cheeks and her forehead.

"Cecile! You actually came all the way here! I can't believe it."

"But of course. I couldn't miss this!" She strangles me with a hug. We sway back and forth as a larger crowd is gathering.

Hans taps my shoulder. "Karl, meet all your well-wishers. There are people here from all over Europe as well as Asia. One person even came up from Africa!" I release Cecile and I turn to greet the crowd. Bernard puts a beer in my hand.

I'm shocked at the turnout. I just walk the line and say, "Hi, I'm Tommy."

"Reginald, mate!"

"Marta."

"Fredrick."

"Amber."

"Dara."

"Bodhi."

"Muhammed."

"Jabari."

"Alexa."

"Karina."

"Antonio."

"Anka."

"Anna."

Cecile comes back over to me with her smiling, carefree self. "What do you say, Tommy? Let's eat!"

I'm looking around at all of the faces. People I have never met. Invested enough in my journey that they are willing to spend their holiday with me. And old friends that I will miss dearly. I inhale. I exhale. "Okay! Let's get this party started! Drinks are on me!"

27

PHENOMENON

My luggage is checked in at the counter and having cleared security I have an hour or so before the metal *Nachtkrapp* takes me home. I am browsing pictures I posted on Oratr from the initial stages of my journey. There is little resemblance between the image of this *cœur trieste* and the *nowa dusza* I see in the mirror today. Obscured in self-imposed darkness, the former is vague and muted. Smiles are premeditated, and self-doubt is innate. Every beam of visible light is external. Inside there is emptiness. Okay, maybe that is a little much but it seems that way. My pity for him is so overwhelming and I almost forget that bedeviled sap is me. The weight that is deforming his posture is pathetic. On his left shoulder, I can see an imprint from Katrina's head. On his right, Jacob's hand rests like supergravity. Dreary fool. Like a blind mule carrying a load of misery and wish-it-were through a hostile desert.

I'm nearing the end of the concourse. I will be boarding flight 1609. Soon, I will be out of Prague. My year-long expedition will end its last chapter. I sit down and soak in the rumbling Czech sound waves.

~

WHAT THE HELL?

A few seats down from me on the edge of the chair a small object barely remains balanced. I must be hallucinating! My eyes are squinting to maximize details. Yep! That's got to be it. It's a poetic boomerang of sorts. An unbelievable turn of circumstances. Lightly worn edges. A black rectangle decorated with a handwritten red "T" on the flat surface.

That's my wallet!

Without another thought, I leap across the other chairs and grasp the wallet. Unfolding it at the crease gives me a familiar sensation, yet remarkably distant. My index and middle fingers are paired together, and I sweep the inside pocket. It's there. My heart is racing. Katrina's charm!

Time stops briefly and the crowd around me stiffens like storefront mannequins. As the rhythm of my heart steadies and the thumping subsides. Bodies begin to move again. I feel a light tap on my shoulder. I rotate around and standing in front of me is a seemingly respectable man with well-groomed hair and academic-looking glasses. Tugging at his shirt, a bright-faced girl, no more than six years old, sinks her head into the man's jean-covered leg.

"Pardon me, sir, do you speak English?" He is so polite, yet I barely understand him.

"Ah, British! Yes, sir, I speak English."

"I know that looks like rubbish." Ouch! "But, it actually has a special meaning for my daughter." Her face swivels fully into the jeans. I kneel.

"Is this your purse, my lady?"

She reveals the profile of her face and in the undercurrent of airport noise her voice meekly utters, "Uh, huh."

"What is your name?"

"Tabatha." She hides again.

My eyes move back to the gentleman. "That must be what the 'T'is for. Tabatha!"

"It is, with a bit of luck, I suppose. I found the purse displayed on a merchant's rug in Paris. She fell in love with it immediately. We were teaching her how to spell her name and once she discovered the letter 'T,' she insisted on having it."

"Is that so?" I drop my head down again to meet Tabatha's eyes. A huge grin appears on her face and she lets out an innocent giggle. Then, she quickly burrows her face into her father's leg again.

"Yes. And as a bit of a bonus, inside a red horse charm. Tabatha is quite fond of horses and, as it so happens, the color red, I'm afraid. So, it just seemed like the perfect arrangement. She hasn't let it out of her sight since the morning we purchased it. I do not regularly conduct business transactions on the streets–you never know where these chaps get their merchandise–but, I made an exception."

Bzzz. Bzzz. My pocket rattles.

"WELL, Lady Tabatha, I would not dream of keeping you from it any longer." Her face lights up like a candle as I hand it to her.

Bzzz. Bzzz.

AS THESE LOVELY people walk away I check the incoming messages on my phone. I cannot control the smile. Bumps erupt all over my arms. My sensitivity to the air conditioning is heightened and I shiver. Nonetheless, I am thirsty and would like some gum. Perhaps, I will get a drink, a bag of crisps, and gum.

This is the final boarding for KLM flight 1609 to Amsterdam, Gate B12.

A bag of goodies hanging from my hand, I bid the pleasant woman behind the counter adieu in a poor facsimile of the Czech language.

Bzzz. Bzzz.

"*¡Mi amor! ¿Estás bien?* Answer me."

"Boarding plane now." | Send

Bzzz. Bzzz.

"Ok! When do you get back to your mom's?"

"At about 7 or so." | Send

Bzzz. Bzzz.

"Then just a week?"

"Yep." | Send

Bzzz. Bzzz.

"*¿Entonces Colombia?*"

"I can't wait to see you." | Send

• • •

Bzzz. Bzzz.

"Me also. I can't wait to meet *su mama and papa*."

"They are excited, too. Not as much as me." | Send

People. Delightful things. The truth is around us. I guess you have only to learn how to accept change to be able to truly see it. Keep a piece of your heart to feel it; keep a tight hold of your soul to be it. There are always those out there just beyond the horizon looking out for you: a mother, a father, a boss, a kind French friend feasting on living things, three *Arschlöcher* taking on life with confidence, a health nut in perpetual purification reminding you of some fond memory, and a surprise even greater–a slice of paradise with a thick Colombian accent leading you through an apocalypse of animus and into the genesis of peace.

~ End ~

TOMMY'S PATH THROUGH EUROPE

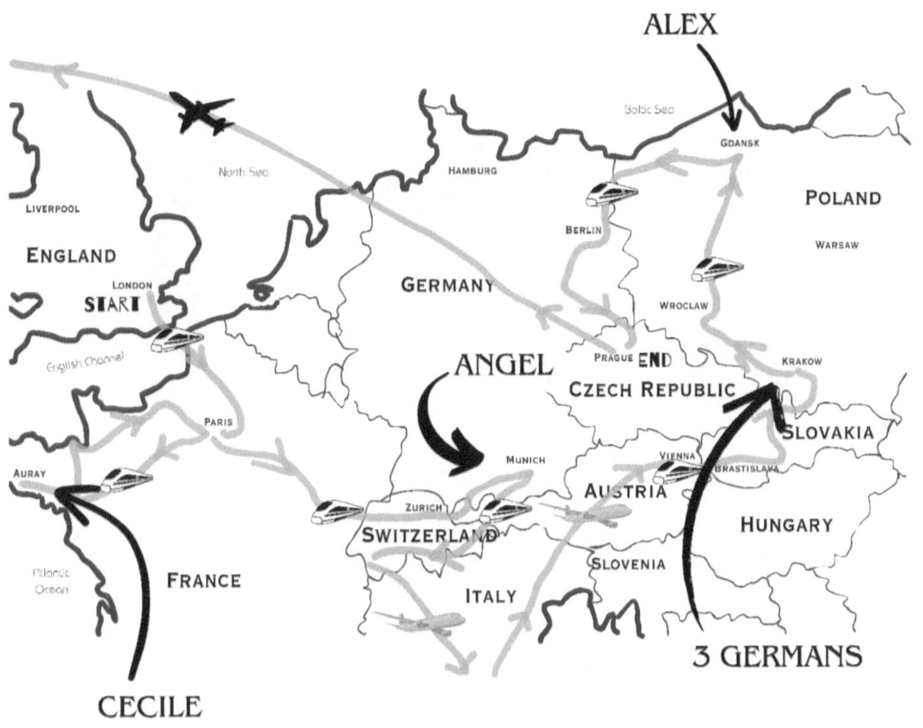

THE ENGLISH (mis)ADVENTURE

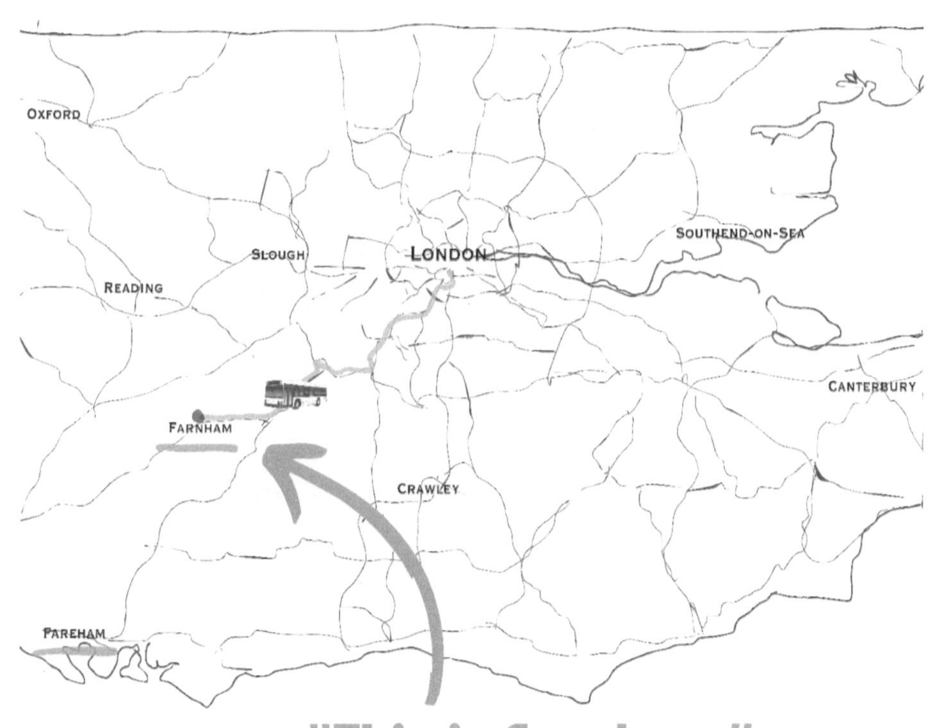

TOMMY'S ORATR ACCOUNT
PRIVATE
^KATRINA
Hey!
^ME
Hello
^KATRINA
Send
BROADCASTS
^7 PM London - Tue
Today I found a great place to eat. (posted)
3
^10 PM London - Tue
Busy day, go! (posted)
2
Post
Logged in as: ^Tommyhawk1
Oratr®
Say something great!
AUDIENCE
9
ACTIVE
7
LIVE
6 HR
LAST
2
ORATIONS
1
WAITING
Edit
Send
New

Photo Credit: Tommy Lopez.

Cecile eating her crepes in Auray, France.

A picture of Angel standing in front of the *Universidad National de Colombia* in Bogotá.

Photo Credit: Unknown.

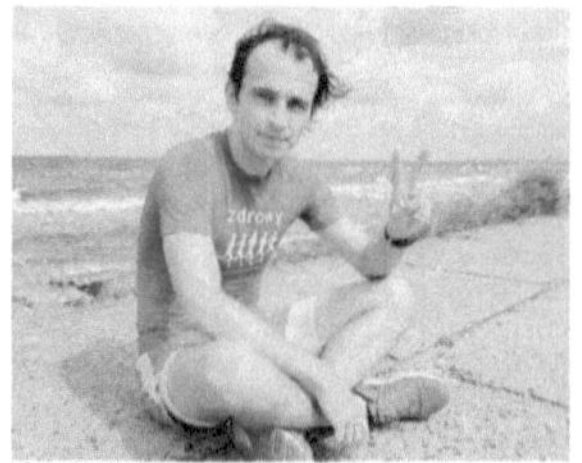

Photo Credit: Tommy Lopez.

Aleksandr posing for a quick picture at the Baltic Sea near Gdańsk, Poland.

Bernard, Hans, and Dietrich continue their antics in the Main Square, Kraków, Poland. Left: Bernard Hoffer of Hamburg. Center: Dietrich Gertz of Bitburg (aka Shitsburg). Right: Hansel "Hans" Krueg of Berlin

Photo Credit: Tommy Lopez.

Photo Credit: Tommy Lopez.

Cecile and Tommy at Le Mont-Saint-Michel, Normandy, France. The water is far away, for now.

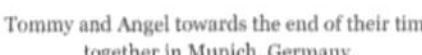

Tommy and Angel towards the end of their time together in Munich, Germany.

Photo Credit: Unknown.

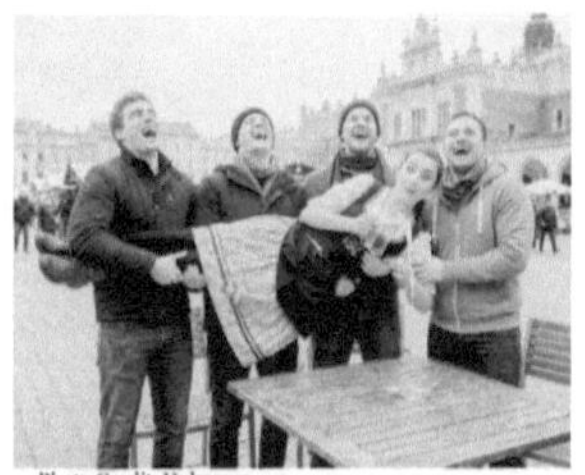

Photo Credit: Unknown

Tommy, Bernard, Hans, Dietrich, and the woman who brought the beer (Zofia) in Kraków, Poland.

A sly fox. Jacques after providing his brand of "hospitality" at Gare de Nord in Paris, France.

Photo Credit: Tommy Lopez.

ABOUT THE AUTHOR

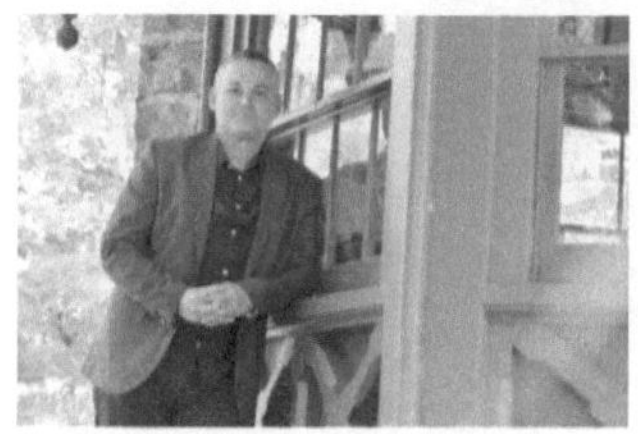

George standing next to Mark Twain's study. Elmira College, Elmira, NY.

George, a multi-generation native of Key West, Florida, brings the vibrant spirit of his hometown to the page. *Meet Me in Prague* marks his debut as an author. He holds an M.A. in English from the University of West Florida, where he developed his passion for storytelling and literature.

www.ingramcontent.com/pod-product-compliance
Lightning Source LLC
Chambersburg PA
CBHW020116310726
48970CB00002B/664

* 9 7 8 1 9 7 1 4 5 4 0 0 9 *